THIS is America?!!

- A European Expat in the USA

Available as a paperback or eBook.

THIS is America?!!

- A European Expat in the USA

by Jonathan Claay

Available as a paperback or eBook.

Other Books by Jonathan Claay:

Rucklingsdorf - An American Surrounded by Germans (English) - available as a paperback or eBook.

Rucklingsdorf - Ein Amerikaner von Deutschen umzingelt (German) - available as a paperback or eBook.

Impressum
© 2019 Jonathan Claay
Herstellung und Verlag:
BoD – Books on Demand, Norderstedt

ISBN: 9783749466344

Book Reviews

"Good ol' fashioned lit'rature!"
   - Jonathan Claay, Book Reader

_____

"I like you *so-o-o-o* much...
  now buy my book
  (after all, that's the *American* way)."
  - Jonathan Claay, Author

_____

"On sale *now*!
  2 for the price of 1 pair!
  What a *deal*!"
  - Jonathan Claay, C.P.O.
    (Chief Promotional Officer)

_____

"This book it HOT!
  And yet... sooo *co-o-o-o-l*."
  - Jonathan Claay, a Regular Guy

Table of Contents

The First Day in the USA

As the door opens, there is an eruption of joy.

"Helloooo, Kai!"

"Welcome to America, Kai!"

"Yeaaaaa!! Kai's here!"

The celebrants have their arms raised, and some are pumping the air with their fists in an excited rhythm, going "whOO, whOO, whOO!". They are surrounded by floating helium balloons printed with ecstatic smiley faces, the word "Congrats!" in confetti-colors and a waving American flag swelling out on the puffy, inflated surfaces.

The balloons are almost indistinguishable among the faces of Kai's new coworkers.

Kai Regenbogen has heard about the Americans, that they can be a bit "over the top" when it comes to expressing themselves, but he had never been confronted with it until now. Facing the unexpected crowd, he remembers when he started in the German branch of the air-defense company just out of college: there was a sociable and respectful round of handshakes, an in-depth description of the department and his awaiting duties, and then some vague chatter before everyone went their separate, quiet ways to their desks.

Now, in his new workplace in America, he cannot help but smile among the infectious energy of this reception they are giving him – as though he is a long-absent family member who has finally returned, with whom they have a shared history, many intimate moments of long-developed trust, and deeply persononal experiences that only they share and over which they can now finally reminisce.

But they are complete strangers.

American strangers.

And that makes all the difference.

Before he can figure out how to respond to this ebullient welcome from people he has never met before, the group suddenly breaks apart and the members stride towards him, like wild molecules of an exploding atom.

He steps back in surprise (and not without a dim sense of fear), but they quickly surround him. The short fat woman in the front of the group is the first to reach up and throw her arms around his upper torso for a big, sloppy hug. The others follow, the men as well as the women, and it is like he has slipped and fallen into an octopus tank. There are arms everywhere, and he is engulfed in the mass of denim and casual wear. His shoulders and back are being patted in different rhythms from all sides... and then they all step back one by one and smile at him, glowing – like happy bunnies, as if expecting something similar in return.

Kai takes a moment to adjust from the shock, not knowing how to respond to such expressiveness from people who, five minutes before, he would have passed on the street without any acknowledgement between them.

Standing still in his private space, the German engineer digs deep into his heart and soul and comes up with a "Sank you, everybody", with a slight smile on his face. He conceives of this as an equivalent reaction on his part to what he has just received, because it is not a phrase that is lightly dispensed in his home culture.

The crowd members are a bit surprised by his subdued reaction. They expected more of a "Hey, everybody! GREAT to be here!", like from a stand-up comedian taking the stage under the glaring spotlights of a nighttime talk show.

Next to him, the smiling Human Resources worker takes up the ball and says, "Kai, as your 'Corporate Ambassador'" – the Americans *love* manipulating language for the sake of hyperbolic effect – "I would like to welcome you to your new family".

He thinks suddenly of the Soviets who took over part of his country decades ago, and who started with a somewhat similar approach.

"We all know you're a long way from your home in –", and the chubby woman with the bare arms and the deeply-unbuttoned shirt looks at the paper on top of her folder "– Bad and Word Embargo?" (she says it like a question, and as though it's hard for her to believe that someone's hometown can have such a peculiar name).

"Baden-Wuerttemberg", Kai says. "Dat vas where I vorked, but I am vrom de Nort of Chermany – a little village called Rucklingsdorf[1]."

---

[1] Kai's hometown of Rucklingsdorf is the subject of another book, which is available in English under the title <u>Rucklingsdorf - An American Surrounded by Germans</u> and in German under the title <u>Rucklingsdorf - Ein Amerikaner von Deutschen umzingelt</u>, both of which are available as eBooks and paperbacks.

"That's a mouthful, dude", says somebody from the crowd. The man is of slightly more than average height, and rather full-formed, but not yet noticeably heavy by local standards. His cheeks are somewhat puffy and he looks as if he has been inflated a bit by a bicycle pump, but he is not known as being comparatively fat.

"Kai Reagan-Bacon, I would like to introduce you to your 'Company Buddy', Jim Macintyre", she says warmly and with a secretive smile, as if introducing Kai to the person whom he has waited for all his life to meet, and as if there is no doubt on anybody's part that this is the beginning of a long, life-altering friendship. "Jim's here to help you get oriented during your new 'Life Challenge' as a new member of our team, and in case you ever just need someone to talk to". She pouts her lips a little as she says this last part, pretending to be sad.

"They call me 'Big Jim'. Howyadoin', buddy!", the heavy man says, taking a step closer and leaning out his open hand for what becomes a sturdy handshake. As Kai smiles wordlessly in respectful response, he is suddenly pulled off-balance by Big Jim's paw and lands with a "THUD" against his "Company Buddy's" chest, where he is given a "Bro" hug.

A "Bro" hug is when two guys (usually Americans) lean their upper torsos together and pat each other roughly on the back of the shoulders, three times quickly, like a boxing referee just before saying "OK, fellas, break it up". Distinctly separate at the hips and legs the entire time, they then step apart, and there is a slightly awkward pause, as if they really aren't sure if they (two males) should in fact

4

be hugging (in spite of having been told since the 1990's that they *should* be doing it), while they stand there and silently worry to themselves about whether what they just did really doesn't mean that they are in fact homosexuals.

To cover all contingencies, the "Bro" hug is sometimes approached from the side, with the two males meanwhile turning their faces away from each other and each stretching to reach a single arm around the other's shoulders, giving the requisite three quick, aggressive "MANLY PATS", and then separating, as if nothing out of the ordinary happened: emotional side expressed, but that doesn't mean I'm gay.

After completing the three hearty pats on the back of Kai's shoulders, Big Jim looks to the crowd of smiling faces (everyone is clearly satisfied with the "good feeling" that has been displayed) and says "OK, let's show this guy how we party in the USA!"

A round of "WHOO, WHOO's" and fist pumps are joined by a sole, rather self-conscious "Yee-Haaa!" as the group cleaves in two to disclose from behind them the table with a sheet cake, several giant bottles of soft drinks and big, red plastic party cups. Big Jim slings his arm around the shoulder of his "Company Buddy" and ushers him to the table. Someone cuts the first piece of cake, which has some of the exclamation point on it from the "Welcome to America Kai!" that is written in bright-red artificial icing across the red-white-and-blue surface.

Everybody takes a piece, and there is an excited flurry of chatter from the high-pitched voices, which sound as if they had all inhaled the helium from the balloons moments before. There is a lot of self-conscious mouth gaping and eyes ripping wide open to express surprise at whatever their current conversant might be telling them at the moment.

Amid the cake party, people now and then jump in spontaneously between Big Jim and Kai and take selfies with them, without any warning. Others take close-ups of themselves and their friends with the cake, and one guy takes a picture just of himself with the rubber plant. The photos are instantly posted to their social media accounts, and the friends who took the pictures together access their social media accounts on their phones to look at the same pictures of themselves, and then they interrupt the people next to them and show them the photos of themselves on their screens. It's quite a party.

In all of the flurry of action, one man, while talking with a coworker, accidentally bumps into a female coworker from behind. He suddenly turns around with a look of horror on his face and shouts "Oh, excuse me! I didn't mean to bump into you!", loud enough for everyone to hear, his hands and forearms now raised distinctly in the air for all to see, as if trapped in an alley by a police force, as he looks around at everyone for some sort of confirmation that they recognize his innocence. Everybody stops talking and looks, evaluates the situation, and then returns to their chatter, as if nothing worthy of further action has occurred.

There are smiles and loud, squealing laughs, with mouths stretching as wide as possible, like someone preparing to stuff in a cheeseburger that might just be able to fit, with a little effort. The women are heavily layered with make-up – eye shadow, eye liner, rouge, pancake foundation – and the entire event seems like an amateur performance for a camera that everybody imagines is filming them; they laugh the moment they find a reason to justify doing so, and the laughs are big, loud laughs, with a lot of arching and plunging of the eyebrows, like when adults talk to children and exaggerate their facial expressions to get the point across.

After the initial performances, the "Corporate Ambassador" from the Human Resources department looks at her watch and says, "Well, everybody, it looks like it's time for Kai to get his first tour of his new 'Company Home'".

As they raise their plates and cake forks and all say "Bye!" in a disjointed unison, one coworker says "Bye, Kai!", and then immediately turns to her friends and repeats her discovered rhyme of "Bye, Kai!", as if the humor of it is overwhelming, and they all start screaming at each other in varying degrees in appreciative laughter, like wild creatures screeching together on a hilltop.

The "Corporate Ambassador" from the HR department laughs as she gestures to Kai that they should be leaving. She continues laughing to her colleagues as she backs herself out of the area (it is more a wide-eyed dropping of the jaw with the lips pulled back as far as possible to expose the teeth, as if she might bite at any moment, out of pure joy).

Then, she and the new worker from overseas walk down the hall to begin their tour of the premises.

"This is our 'Paris Bistro'", she says, gesturing grandly as they approach the sign above the company canteen. The sign has the requisite pictures of a baguette, an accordion and a puffy chef's hat. There is a salad bar, a few items warming in cafeteria trays, and a snack stand filled with candy bars and chips. "You'll probably feel right at home here, since you're from Europe and all".

The Human Resources "Corporate Ambassador" looks up at Kai eagerly, with wide, almost pleading eyes, wringing her hands together tightly at her chest, as if awaiting some kind of confirmation that the elegance of the establishment is as effective as intended, particularly to this authentic person from... from Almost-France.

"Charming", he offers, in an effort to be diplomatic.

Her mouth opens into a smile of relief. "We knew you'd like it", she gasps, as if it had been built just for him, when the sign was installed two years ago.

They continue on with their tour to what looks like a children's play room. There are brightly-colored beanbag chairs sagging like whipped cream here and there on the carpeted floor. There are two men playing at a foosball table; amongst the desperate banging and knocking of the game, one of the men whips his wrist suddenly and there is the hollow wooden sound of the ball banging sharply around into the goal, followed by a hard, aggressive "HAAAAA!!" by the victor, as if he has just brutally destroyed his opponent and stolen from him his last breath. There is also a pool table, as well as a juice bar and, of course, a snack machine.

8

This is our "Chill Zone", the Human Resources representative says. She says it with her eyes half closed, and with her hand bent flat horizontally, drawing a line in front of her from left to right, as if she is stoned. After this rendition, she laughs at Kai again.

"Is this for after work?", Kai asks.

"Oh, no no", she says, worried at the misunderstanding, "All our salaried staff members can come here at any time, and just "Chill Out"!", she says, making the gesture again, followed by the same laugh, as though she has been reading from the same script.

"We also have a laundry area, a bath with showers, and a 'Nap Zone' for sleepy heads", she chirps, bending her head onto her folded hands and closing her eyes, to perform for him her rendition of the act of napping. Then she lifts herself into a professional posture and adds, "We gratefully offer these little perks to ensure that our salaried staff members achieve a healthy and satisfying work-life balance", repeating the key words from a PowerPoint slide show presented in her department last year by the HR manager. The presentation was entitled "Employee Retention – Easy and Breezy".

What she doesn't mention to Kai today is the factoid that the employees generally work from 60 to 80 hours per week and don't have time to go home to pursue the daily luxuries of bathing, doing laundry and sleeping.

They walk along the hall between a row of white office-room doors on one side and the giant external glass wall on the other, through which – across the little triangular patch of well-manicured grass – another row of white office-doors can be seen in the other wing of the building.

As they stroll along, she asks Kai the vague, all-encompassing question of "So, what's it like to live in Europe?".

"Vat is it like? In *Europe?*", Kai says, wondering how he can possibly begin to respond.

After a bewildered pause, he starts by stating the population of the city in Germany where he last worked, and then he begins to list its most prominent monuments.

All the while, the "'Corporate Ambassador'" nods her head up and down, with her mouth gaping a little, saying "Uh huh… uh huh…" at evenly dispersed intervals. Her eyes are targeted unwaveringly at him as he talks, but they start to blur a little.

Kai looks at her from time to time, not entirely sure that the person who asked the question and is nodding at him is actually listening to what he is saying.

They have come some distance from the other areas that he has been shown, and from the direction in which they are heading, he starts to hear a sound of white noise. It is constant, rather high pitched, and frenetic.

As they approach, it becomes clear that the sound is composed of layer upon layer of different screams: some sharp and sudden, some long and drawn out, more like yelling. They come nearer to a doorway that is painted in bright red, blue and yellow color fields, and there is a painting of a giraffe next to the entrance. It is as if the door is pounding and flexing outwards, bulging at its hinges with the yelling and screaming from inside.

Through the glass insert in the door, Kai sees a mass of children running wildly and throwing stuffed animals and pillows around the room. Some are chasing each other, others are being chased, a few are crying, and one little girl with short, blonde hair is sitting on the floor, Indian-style, with her elbows pressed into her legs and pouting, as if the world about her has collapsed.

"That's our 'Kiddie Care'", the Human Resources "Corporate Ambassador" informs him. "We offer our salaried staff a full child care program, so that parents can be sure that their little ones are always safe and happy, even while Mommy and Daddy are *hard at work*" (as she says the last words, she clenches her fists and presses her facial features together, as if in parody of being *hard at work*, and to convey the image that, compared to what she has just shown, nobody at their company really works *that* hard, and so everything is therefore really just cool.

"Do you have any children who might need to enjoy the benefits of our '"Kiddie Care" services, Kai?"

The European expat bends forward and peeks through the glass once more. He sees a fat boy standing on a stool and reaching into the fish tank, trying to squeeze the fish.

"No", Kai says. "No sank you."

————————————————

At his desk a few hours later, Kai has started on his first chores in his new position. He is reading over some papers from a file folder, and then he gets up and walks down the hall to the copy room.

On his way, he passes an open door where people are gathered around a cake on a rolling metal trolley, and everybody in the room suddenly shouts "Happy Birthday!" and starts singing. The woman they are singing to turns around in her chair and opens her eyes and mouth wide in surprise. As they sing, she looks as if she is going to cry.

He walks on and reaches the copy room. He turns the corner to enter, and then stops suddenly and says, "Oh, hello. Exkoos me."

One of his coworkers from another department is at the copy machine. She is wearing thin office trousers, which look professional, but still allow the shape of her hips, buttocks and thighs to be noticeable. The sleeves of her blouse end high on her shoulders and the top button starts somewhere dangerously near her abdomen.

"Hi!", she says to the young man with the foreign accent who is standing behind her, just inside the door. She has turned her head toward him, but her body is still facing the copy machine, and she starts to lean on it a bit. "I won't be long", she says, smiling at him over her shoulders.

"That is OK", Kai says, returning the smile, and…

… a hand suddenly appears firmly on his bicep from behind, and he is pulled sharply outside of the room, as if the hand has rescued him out of a surging sea.

It is a young man whom he has never seen before. Without stopping as he continues to walk past, and without even looking at Kai, the man gestures with his head towards the woman and the copy room, and he simply states the words "lawsuit, dude", and he walks on.

Kai watches the man walk away, and then turns to the copy room, confused.

"I...I sink I vill joost come back again later", he says to the woman.

"OK, bye", she says, smiling at him attentively over her shoulder.

He smiles politely and returns to his office space.

At his desk, he notices that his upper back is starting to ache a little. It is from the air conditioning, which makes the air so cold that it has become a bit unpleasant.

He gets up and goes to the window, and he looks all around the edges of it for a fixture of some kind, whereby he can open the window to "warm down" a little.

Finding none, he starts to push at the glass lightly, trying to budge it.

"Wassup?", asks one of his colleagues.

"Oh, it is a bit cool for me. I wanted to open a window, to get zzum fresh air."

"The windows don't open", his coworker says, "They're made of a special bullet-proof glass".

Kai's eyes open suddenly.

"But don't worry 'bout it, man", his coworker adds. "The indoor climate is controlled to ensure perfect ambient conditions." It's a quotation from another PowerPoint slide show.

Kai looks at the window. There is a fly buzzing about frantically in the bottom corner, smashing its body against the clear glass pane in a desperate and futile effort to escape. Just across from the fly, on the counter, there is a little American flag protruding from a stand. On the stand, there are the words "Born Free!" in thick, gold-painted lettering.

"But yad betta get yer junk off the window sill, there", the man gestures to Kai's stapler and pen dispenser. "The shades open and close automatically with the sun."

Kai looks perplexedly at his coworker, then just as perplexedly at the vertical louvered window shades.

"I see", he says, and then "Sank you", as he smiles to his coworker.

He moves his things to his desk, makes a mental note to always bring a sweater to the office from now on, and then returns to his work.

After a while, he looks up to see someone smiling warmly as she enters and brings a baby to one of the women who is working at another desk across the room. The seated woman smiles as she takes the baby, and the ladies chat as the mother at the desk opens her shirt, cups her hand to lift out her breast, and starts to breast-feed her child.

Kai keeps looking: at the child's mouth, at the woman's beast that rhythmically disappears into and reappears from it, and at the two women as they chat casually.

After a few moments, the woman who has brought in the baby looks fixedly and rather sternly at Kai. Noticing that he has inadvertently been staring at them, he recoils a bit, smiles to them, and returns to his computer screen.

The women continue chatting.

After a while, from the corner of his eye, the German expatriate sees the contented child being removed from the woman's arms. The mother wipes her breast with a cloth and closes her blouse, but not before a drop of milk falls onto the business documents in front of her.

'I wonder if that makes the ink run', Kai wonders to himself, being sure not to look directly at her. 'I hope it is nothing important.'

————————————————

After a few hours, feeling a bit light headed from his work, Kai gets up from his desk and goes down the hall to a snack machine.

The chocolate bars are all filled with one sort of gooey mixture or another, and the bright designs on the packaging all make it look like the chocolate bars are about to explode. The chocolate is all pale milk chocolate; there is no selection that contains the rich, dark chocolate that Kai always ate back in Germany.

"You ready, dude? I'm starving", says a voice behind him. It's a man about his age.

"Oh, go ahead", says Kai, gesturing a clear path to the machine. "I cannot make up my mind."

"Know what ya' mean… it *all* looks good", says the man. He shoves a coin into the machine and pushes the button for his selection, and after the coin lands inside, one of the chewy chocolate bars makes a "BUNK" sound as it lands in the dispenser.

As soon as he takes the chocolate out, the man rips the wrapper open and chomps into it, eating half of it at one time as he stands there and leans against the machine.

"I'm soooo hungry", he says out loud.

Kai looks at the chocolate bar and at the man chewing and says "I know vat you mean."

The man suddenly stands upright, wipes his right hand back and forth on the front of his shirt, and sticks it out to Kai and says, "Hi, I'm Zack".

Kai smiles and shakes his hand, "Hi… Sack? I'm Kai."

"It's Zack, short for Z-z-zackary", and he wiggles his head back and forth on his neck, as if pretending a very serious person is saying something very important.

"Oh, hello Zack. It is nice to meet you."

"Me too, man. What's yer name again? Kite?"

"Kai, and it is not short for anysing, I am afraid".

"That's cool", Zack says.

At the mentioning of the word "cool", Kai remembers his upper back and the air conditioning.

The American is so casual and friendly, though, that his German colleague can't help but feeling relaxed and welcome.

"What is your department?", Kai asks.

"Oh, I'm a contractor," Zack says, looking away.

"A contractor?", Kai repeats. "Do you work in the legal department?"

"No!", Zack says, laughing easily. "I'm on contract here. I don't have a regular job. I get a contract for three months, and if I don't burn the place down, they might gimme another contract after that one."

"Oh", says Kai, suddenly becoming aware of the financial predicament the other man is in.

"Yea. I'm on my second contract so far. After a year, they might give ya' a 'Bronze' contract. That's for six months."

"Well, that is better than three months", Kai says, with a look of empathy for his colleague.

"Yea. Or they might not gimme anything at all", Zack says, raising his eyebrows. "But I'm doin' alright", he suddenly adds, waxing optimistic. "I drive for Lyft on the weekends, and between that and rentin' out the other room in my apartment on Airbnb, I can get by."

Kai pauses, trying to say something kind to this man who seems to be living so close to the edge, in spite of working with him in this international company.

"Maybe zey will hire you here full time in de future", Kai says.

Zack breathes deeply and looks out down the hallway into the distance. "Prob'ly not. But no sweat. I just work here for my candy money!", he says, raising the candy bar as he takes a last chomp of it. Then, he throws the empty wrapper into the garbage pail and wipes his hands together, as though he is through with it. He looks at Kai and has a big smile on his face, in spite of the story he has just told.

"Well, it was great talkin' to ya', man… Kai, right?"

"Exactly. Kai. And you're Zack, for Zackary."

"Excellent!", and Zack raises his hand for a high five.

Kai pauses, and then slowly raises his hand to meet the other, and Zack gives his a hearty "SMACK" and says "Alri-i-i-ight".

Zack looks like he wants to say more, but as if he doesn't know how to go about it, so he says "Well, I gotta get back to work. I don't want this place to fall apart without me! See ya, Kai."

"See you, Zack! Have a good day", the German expat says, and he watches the young man disappear down the hall.

Then, Kai turns to the snack machine, selects a little bag of pretzels, and walks slowly back to his open-plan room where his desk is, remembering what Zack told him.

'Three months', he thinks to himself.

After he has been working at his computer for a while, the woman from the Human Resources office who had given him his tour of the building enters the room with a file in her hands.

"Hi, Kai. As your 'Corporate Ambassador', I just wanted ta' come by and see how it's goin'. So… howzitgoin'?".

"Oh, very well, sank you. I had a pleasant chat with Zack a little while ago."

The woman's face starts to show signs of underlying disturbance.

"Zackary?"

"Yes, Zackary", Kai says, smiling at the recollection of the pleasant encounter.

"Ri-i-i-ight", the "'Corporate Ambassador'" says, looking down. Then she perks up, as if ready to recite her next loop of corporate jargon.

"Zackary is one of our 'Visiting Staff' members. He doesn't have a regular contract, like you and me", and she smiles to Kai and leans a little closer to him as she says this, as if sharing a secret bond with him.

"Actually", Kai says, "he said that he vas a contract worker."

The HR rep looks a little frustrated, but retains her composure and her corporate persona as she explains the situation as cautiously and professionally as she can.

"Our industry has a fluctuating demand, and to ensure that we are able to meet our client's requirements at all times, we occasionally secure the services of ancillary service providers", she says.

Kai nods as he listens, and she sees that she has to go further.

"The ancillary staff are not entitled to the same perks that we offer our salaried staff, like *you*, Kai", she says, a wide, open-mouthed smile suddenly blossoming between her jangling ear-rings.

Kai is still listening, so she tries to get to the point.

"Most of our full-time workers prefer to socialize with their full-time colleagues. They seem to think that they have more in common," and she smiles again at the nice idea of people having things in common.

"I see", Kai says, and smiles politely to her.

"Hey, buddy!"

It's Big Jim Macintyre.

"You're not trying to steal this guy away to another department, are you?", Big Jim says with playful sternness to the HR representative. "He's doing a *great* job so far!", and he smiles at Kai, who smiles back at the compliment.

"No, no!", she says. "Kai's staying right where he is. Don't you worry about *that*."

"Great! We're just starting up a project with a major air defense client, and we need Kai to help us protect the greatest country in the word!", Big Jim says, beaming with pride.

"Where is that?", Kai asks innocently.

The two people standing at his desk frown as they look down at him.

"Oh!", Kai says. "Of course!".

And his shoulders twitch suddenly as a light, mechanical "Whirr" sounds behind him. It's the vertical louvers of the shade, as they start to automatically extend across the window to block out the bright sun.

The Comforts of Home

On his first Saturday in America, Kai Regenbogen has been invited to the home of his "Company Buddy", Big Jim Macintyre.

"How'd ya' like ta' come by tomorrow afternoon and see how real Americans live, right up close and personal?", is the way Big Jim phrased the invitation the day before in the office. He had a big smile on his face, and he was already leaning forward a bit, ready to give Kai a slap on the back of the shoulders and flood him with a hearty "Yeee-aaaaa!" right after the acceptance, which is exactly what followed.

While the invitation is not exactly required by "Corporate Policy", it *is* mentioned near the top of the list in the "Good Ideas!" memo that is sent when a worker is about to begin upon his "new journey" of being a "Company Buddy" (and that "journey" definitely looks good on one's record when bonuses are discussed in the "Employee Review" each year).

As Kai pulls up to the curb on Saturday in his moderately-sized green hybrid, he sees Big Jim out on the front lawn. Jim is wearing shorts that go half-way down his legs, his T-shirt hanging loose over his stomach, and he is tugging at a garden hose, scowling defiantly at the place where it is caught on one of the stepping stones that lead around the house.

As Kai closes his car door and walks up the driveway, Big Jim's contracted facial features suddenly morph into those of a welcoming party host, his eyes expanding and his mouth opening wide, like a thick toad trying to catch flies.

"Hey, dude! You *made* it!", as if a great challenge has been overcome and Kai's great times are only now about to begin.

Jim throws down the loops of the garden hose. It's a complicated release, like freeing one's fingers from molasses, and he frowns angrily at the adversarial hose once again until he is free of its insolent grasp.

"Welcome to my castle!", Big Jim says, putting his arm around his guest's shoulder and walking with him to the front door (Jim had been sweating a bit from the garden work, and Kai can feel it through his shirt).

It's a somewhat large house, or rather, it's laid out to look somewhat larger than it actually is: there are various rooms, piled one upon the other like boxes, with some protruding forward and some recessed, like the contours of a fat woman in a thin dress.

Kai tries to place the architectural style in his mind: supporting the overhang above the front entrance with its Antebellum flair, there is a simplified version of two classic Greek columns, with swirling rococo decorations at the base and head, as well as gothic ornamentation around the windows. It looks like a "Greatest Hits" pop collection of architectural history.

"Did you design the house?", Kai asks tentatively.

"No, it was built when the rest of the development was put in", Jim says. "But it's a beaut, ain't it?"

The German expat isn't sure whether the house is actually "abeut" or not "abeut", so he looks at the foundation to check that it's level, and then he says, "Yes, it seems to be."

Big Jim releases the hearty laugh that he had been holding in for whatever response would come.

As they come closer to the front door, Kai notices a discolored patch on one of the columns. Seeing his guest notice the flaw, Big Jim says, "Oh, that's just a little accident we had here a while back."

It turns out that one day a few months ago, Big Jim had let his son, Bart, celebrate his 15th birthday by letting him drive the family Sports Utility Vehicle around the block a couple of times. After the boy backed into the driveway following the adventure, his father turned to him from the passenger seat and said, "Not bad, son. Soon you'll be cartin' a whole buncha girls around with ya' in this thing", and the boy smiled at his father – but the boy's foot slipped off the break, and the giant vehicle lurched backwards like a wild bull into the house front, leaving a thick gouge in one of the columns.

Jim leaves some of the details out when recounting the story, but he ends by saying, "Pretty bad ding. Had to patch it up myself with some new paint."

He is smiling as he nods his head up and down, looking from the patch to his new buddy and then back again – clearly quite proud of his skills as a craftsman, in spite of the color difference. "You could see all the way through the Styrofoam," he says.

'Styrofoam?', the German visitor thinks, as an image of his own home from childhood suddenly surges to mind: it was a solid little red brick house, like the responsible one of the three little pigs would build. In the fairy tale, there is of course a house built of straw, and another of sticks, but there is no mention of any house made of Styrofoam.

The host guides his guest through the entrance with his hand on his upper back, much like American politicians do to visiting heads of state in news videos – which might be where Jim got the idea from in the first place.

As they enter, Kai notices the aroma of baking, tainted with the smell of something having been recently burnt.

Distracted by the aroma, he is completely unsuspecting as he suddenly hears a vociferous "BAWF!" in front of him and feels the two thick paws on his chest, shoving him off balance from sheer force of weight.

"DOWN, Rock!, *DOWN!!*", Big Jim shouts domineeringly at the black-and-brown Rottweiler that has just lunged at the guest. "SIT!", Jim shouts threateningly into the animal's face, with an index finger raised firmly in warning. "I said SIT!!"

And the Rottweiler whimpers and paces back and forth before settling into a tenuous posture on its haunches, at which Jim breaks into a big smile as he roughly scrubs the top of the dog's thick head and says, "GOOD dog, Rock. *GOOD* dog!".

Big Jim turns to Kai, who is nervously uncertain of just how much control his host has upon his powerful, rambunctious minion, and whether or not he himself will suddenly be pounced upon again by the corpulent animal with no warning.

"Don't worry, Rock's OK. He wouldn't hurt a fly", Jim says, noticing his guest's anxious appearance. Then, the host crouches down to his pet and rubs his hand quickly, back and forth, across the dog's head again and says, "Would, ya', Rock? Huh?", in answer to which the dog just gapes his mouth and lets his heavy pink tongue unfurl and flap around, loose and uncontrolled.

Kai notices how moist the inside of the dog's mouth is, and he can't stop staring at the pointy teeth projecting solidly from among the dark, black lining of the gums.

From his crouched position beside the dog, Jim looks up with a concerned look at Kai, and then shouts up at his guests' face without looking away, "Hon, why doncha let Rock out in the backyard for a while?"

"You bet!", Jim's wife, Wendy, calls out, stepping in front of the breakfast bar. Then, she yells at the dog "Rock! Commere, boy. How 'bout goin' intathe yard for a while, hey boy?"

And she snaps her fingers several times at the dog's eye level, at which the dog leaps like a tripped spring and rotates, lunging from its meaty haunches as if in hot pursuit as Wendy opens the sliding glass door, quickly steps out of the way of the galloping beast, and then slides the door shut with a loud "Flump!" once the dog has passed through.

Wendy smiles at her husband.

"Thanks, hon", Jim says. Then, to his guest, he adds, "Rock's got a lotta energy", shaking his head from side to side, in amazement at the tremendous amount of energy the dog possesses.

For the first time, Kai has a chance to take a look at his surroundings.

Without stepping any further into the house from where they entered, they are already well into the "Great Room", a euphemism for the single room consisting of entrance hall, living room, kitchen, breakfast bar, and dining area that is so common in modern American homes. If the rooms were partitioned from each other, their congested size would be stifling. Liberated from their boundaries as they are, though, they seem, together, somehow larger than they actually are.

As for furnishing, the room looks like page six from an IKEA catalog: everything is brand new, without a single sign of wear, and nothing is outdated. It looks like the couch, television and easy chair are replaced regularly, once a new trend hits the market.

Kai wonders how such luxury can be afforded on the salaries from the company.

In place of artwork on the walls, there are photographs of the family members, including one of Big Jim and his son holding up a fish in a row boat, as well as a shot of the entire family – Jim and his wife with their son and daughter – in the stands of a football game, with Jim standing up and screaming fiercely as he raises aloft his giant, electric-green foam sports-fan-finger.

The photos are next to a window on the left, through which Kai can see directly into the bedroom of the house next door, which is only a few feet away: the neighbors are installing a set of shelves above the bed this afternoon.

"So, you're *finally* here, Kai!", Wendy says. She says it as if she had been looking forward to his arrival all morning, even though he arrived punctually at the agreed time.

She rushes to the breakfast bar and reaches behind a bowl filled with plastic fruit and a few artificial flowers. She picks up a plastic serving plate from the counter, and holds it up before herself as she walks towards him, like a child raising something aloft for everyone to see.

It's a plate of cookies. They're a little dark, but still warm.

"I just made them myself!", Wendy spurts out gleefully.

Behind her, on the kitchen counter, Kai can see the wrapper from the "Ready-to-Bake!" cookie dough – as well as signs of a recent culinary struggle.

Jim jumps right in and takes one from the top of the pile. Still chewing, he opens his mouth and says to his wife, "Great, honey!", and then he gestures his head from Kai to the cookie platter and says, "Dig in, man. Don't be shy".

As Jim smiles, Kai can see from his host's teeth that the cookies are chocolate.

The expat takes a cookie from the platter and smiles slightly as he says "Sank you" to his hostess, who is radiating with glee that her homemade creation is being so well received.

Kai takes his first bite. Though the outside is dark and crispy, the inside is still chewy and a little undercooked. After he swallows, his mouth feels covered with a layer of some sort of chemical sweetener. He takes another bite to wash away the sensation, but the reprieve only lasts for a moment, and then the taste of the coating returns.

"Wendy *lo-o-o-ves* to cook, don't you, honey?".

"Sure do, whenever I get the chance."

"Me, too", Jim adds, not to be outdone. "I make a *killer* four-alarm chili. But I'll *never* tell anybody the secret – except maybe my son, when he turns 18."

American men generally feel a swaggering pride when it comes to their personal chili recipe. They talk about it as though the recipe is stored in a hidden vault somewhere under the floorboards of the house, together with the family's good jewelry and the mortgage documents – even though, considering the basic ingredients involved, their brilliant creation can't really be so different from the one-of-a-kind chili recipe of every other guy's in the housing development – coupla onions, and a shot of "José's Flamin' Taco Sauce", "Flamin' José's Taco Sauce" or some other commercial preparation (all available right next to each other in aisle seven of the local supermarket).

"It's too strong for me", Wendy leans in to tell Kai, in a whisper that is purposefully loud enough so that everybody in the room can hear it, but so that there is still the air of a secret about it.

Jim's chest expands noticeably as he says, "I usually make it when it's just the guys over."

"It must be ffery powerfol", the German guest says, realizing that such a comment is expected of him.

"Just like Jim is", Wendy says, and as she pats her husband's upper arm, Jim pretends to flex his muscles like a body builder, before breaking out into laughter.

And Wendy laughs along with him.

And the two look at their guest, waiting for him to join in, so that they can all laugh together.

Kai looks back at them and smiles lightly, quietly nodding his head.

They laugh louder, apparently trying to crank-start him, and not knowing why the normal American routine is suddenly not working.

Noticing that something is expected, Kai says, "I guess zat is why zey call him 'Big Jim'", and Jim and his wife bust into the grateful laugh that they had been waiting to make, and they are visibly relieved.

"Common, Kai, check the place out", Jim says, as he turns and starts to walk through the Great Room.

Without saying anything, Jim looks at the entertainment center and smiles, as if wanting to call his guest's attention to it.

In the center of the structure, there is a mammoth, high-definition television, which seems to be hovering in the room like a giant, winged creature, ready to strike – it is visible from all areas of the room (including the entrance), and is clearly the center of attention in the household.

On the shelf below it, there is a multi-colored array of DVD's, with some crammed in on top of the pile, due to lack of space.

'That's where the books would go', Kai can't help but notice.

Satisfied with the impression that he is making on his guest, Big Jim leads Kai to the sliding glass door and gestures with his head to the patio. Through the glass, along with seeing the Rottweiler galloping frantically from one end of the lawn to the other, Kai notices a table with a mosaic surface and four wrought-iron chairs. The set is overly ornamental, and looks like it might be found in a café – not a café in Europe, exactly, but rather one in EuroDisney.

"Ya' like that table and chairs?", Jim asks his guest.

Becoming accustomed at this point to what is socially expected of him in his new country, Kai responds, "It is very nice."

Big Jim smiles at him as if about to expose a secret: "259 at StuffCo", he says, grinning as he nods his head up and down at the amount he paid.

"Oh?", says the European, still at a loss as to how he should handle this one.

"*Great* purchase!", Jim radiates.

"Yes, dat *iss* a good purchase", Kai politely repeats.

Kai had not yet been aware of the great value that Americans place upon making a "good deal" – even if that good deal is printed on a sticker and advertised to anybody in the local population of thousands who are willing to pay exactly the same price, and even though the price is absolutely not negotiable.

They feel as if they have gotten something out of the transaction – gotten a little more for giving a little less. It's like it was with horse traders in America hundreds of years ago, although there was a subtlety in the handling and the negotiation of such deals back then. There was the fear of the deal breaking apart and the other guy taking his horse and going home, and your family starving to death because they wouldn't be able to get to town to buy basic provisions. There was the knowledge that if you paid that extra couple of bucks, you might not have enough money for the coming winter, when the kids might get sick and need medicine. It was a poker game and the stakes were survival, and it called for all of one's sharp skills of haggling and dealing, to make sure that you got ahead and you didn't leave a single morsel on the negotiation table that might keep your family alive for another month on the bitter, windy prairie.

Now, Americans go to the local supercenter, look at the price, see that it has been crossed out with a red marker with the words "10% discount!" added, and they feel just as accomplished as if they were that horse-trader a few hundred years ago.

What's amazing is that they feel this pride in a good deal even if their ancestors just arrived in the country one generation before. After all, this is America, and once they and their family have settled into place, they adapt these characteristics of the club that is the United States. Wherever their ancestors have come from, if they go into a store and make a "good purchase", they are getting ahead, they are *winning* – and that is what it's all about.

The phone rings suddenly. Wendy reaches to the phone unit and smacks the "speaker" button.

"Hi there!", a voice on the phone calls out with eager joy. "How would you like to be lounging at the beach *right now*?!" (it's a robocall – one of the endless slew of automatic marketing calls that disturb American households day after day, particularly during dinner hours). Just as automatically, Wendy reaches to click the call away, when the voice calls out into the Great Room, "*Timeshares* at the *Breaking Surf Lagoon*! Take advantage of our *Summer Sale*, but act *quick,* before it's *too late*!".

At this sales pitch, Wendy lets her finger hover a moment over the disconnect button, and she raises her eyes to meet those of her husband, who is likewise paying sharp attention to the offer and weighing the possibilities.

After an extended pause, he grimaces and shakes his head from side to side, his wife matches his grimace, and in this moment they share a kind of hatred for the robocall and the scam in which they are sure it is trying to catch them.

She smashes the disconnect button with the pad of her index finger more forcefully than is necessary, and the voice of the robocall is interrupted in the middle of its hysterically excited and overly-optimistic "Don't *miss out* on our *fantastic…* booooooooooooop".

As if nothing out of the ordinary has happened, Jim reaches down to the table between the sofa and the entertainment center. Next to the accumulation of remote controls, there is a present.

Jim takes it and holds it out to his guest.

"Here's a little something from all of us, from your new family here (and he gestures to his wife) as well as your new family at work!"

It's a long, thin package, and the wrapping is covered with various iterations of the word "Welcome!" in bulging letters and various colors, all expressing jubilation and exuberance is one way or another.

The German engineer takes the present, thanks his guests humbly and looks at the package. He then turns it over slowly and carefully, as if it is an explosive device that first needs to be defused. Finding the seam, he slides a fingernail under the clear tape and proceeds to methodically release the bond of the adhesive from the surface of the wrapping paper, without the paper suffering any damage in the process.

Big Jim is meanwhile standing across from him, shifting back and forth in place, patting the sides of his upper thighs and tapping his fingers. His puffs up his cheeks and then presses the air out slowly.

As Kai rotates the package and inspects the side for the next location of the adhesive tape, Jim casts a glance at his wife, who returns the glance with her eyes popping in unspoken significance, and then her husband lunges at the package.

Engulfed in the performance of his meticulous procedure, Kai suddenly feels the package yanked from his grip, and he watches as Big Jim r-r-r-ips and tears at the wrapping paper with a wild energy. Colorful shreds with "Welc", "elco" and "ome!" are hurled up into the air and float gracefully down along Big Jim's thick legs, the peaceful freefall of the paper in stark contrast to the wrathful frenzy with which the host is shredding the carefully-wrapped gift package.

Wendy fixes a hanging lock of her hair into place and looks out through the sliding door.

The rampage concluded, Big Jim then lifts the package robotically upwards and then outwards in two separate movements and hands it back to Kai, with an overly self-conscious exhalation of breath, as if to mock the intensity of what he has just done.

Once again, Jim is peaceful and friendly, as if he had not just moments ago vivisected the package like a ravenous wolverine.

Kai looks fixedly at his new acquaintance, and then at the exposed present.

It's a box, and on the surface are the words "Gourmet Jelly Joltz" swirling elegantly in silver and gold, against a background of a varied assortment of colored jellybeans.

"Because have they all that fancy food over there in Europe", Big Jim says.

"And we want you to feel at home, now that you're here in America!", Wendy adds from behind the breakfast bar.

Kai looks up from the box and sees Jim smiling self-assuredly, with the confidence that he has gotten *just* the right gift for *just* the right guy.

"Open it!", Jim bubbles with an eager smile.

Removing the cover, Kai exposes a plastic insert tray with several little compartments, each filled to overflowing with jelly beans, with each little pile a different color than the next.

"They all taste like something else!", Jim says, marveling at this coming together of chemistry, cuisine and his very own Great Room.

At the German expatriate's immobility, Jim ruffles around the package in Kai's hands and flips over the cover, where there is a well-organized chart to describe the flavors of the jelly beans that are in each little compartment.

Jim holds up the upturned cover and points to a list below the chart.

"And you can mix them, to get even *more* flavors!"

His mouth is open like that of a circus clown, and Kai can see the red veins in the whites of his eyeballs.

"How *cool* is that ?!", Jim says, turning to his wife, looking for some kind of reaction in the room. She mimics his facial expression back to him and shakes her head up and down, as if to say, "Yea, I know. *Real* cool!".

And he whips his head back to Kai, without lessening the intensity of his gaping smile.

"So you can mix them," the European says, as though he is surprised by the process, though he is actually perplexed that someone has taken the time to create such a product, market it, and then bestow it upon him.

"Yea!", Jim says, basically shouting now in excitement, assuming that the expat's pause is from disbelief that such a miracle of flavor-mixing can actually be achieved my mere mankind, and not that the expat finds the entire premise to be rather offensive to his intellect and basic sense of good taste.

Then Big Jim points to the list on the inside of the box and says, "Look", as if he is going to get to the bottom of this thing and settle the matter once and for all. "Two Corn Dog Yellows + one Mocha Swirl = Popcorn… *POPCORN* !", he yells, inserting his face only inches away from Kai's. "That's *WILD*!!".

The German engineer is definitely not in his element facing this box that is filled with various risks and unknowns, and he looks up from it to his Company Buddy.

"Shall we try it?", he asks, like a child who wants someone else to evaluate the risk for him and tell him what to do.

"Are you kiddin' me, dude? *POPCORN*!!", and Jim pops four Corn Dog Yellows and two Mocha Swirls into his gaping mouth and starts chewing, his eyes fixed on Kai's, as though the two men are now one.

Then, his eyelids rip open, and he screams "WAAAAAAAAAA!!" directly into Kai's face.

Then, Jim turns to his wife, and repeats, "WAAAAAAAAAA!!".

"That tastes like real friggin' *popcorn*!", he adds. "Man, how do they *do* that?!"

Then he looks his guest in the eyeballs and says, "You ready, dude?", as if they are about to go into combat together.

"Uhm, OK, let us see. How vas dat, again? On yellow dog?", says Kai, as he hovers his fingertips indecisively above the top of the magic beans.

Jim sees what he's up against, so he takes the lead. "Two Corn Dog Yellows", he says, plucking them up from the tray, turning Kai's hand over and letting them fall into Kai's palm, "and one – Mocha – Swirl", he adds, separating the words for dramatic impact.

Then Big Jim closes his eyes half way, nods his head up and down and says factually, "Chug it, dude," as though the right time has now come for Kai's voyage into wonder-fulness.

The European picks up one jellybean at a time and starts chewing it, before reaching for the next, and Jim is starting to pulsate and look impatient again.

"They gotta all go in at the same time, man", he says, shaking his head, and twitching his hands and arms, as if he is trying to restrain himself from suddenly cocking his guest's head back and forcing the Jelly Joltz into his throat – for Kai's own sake, as well as for the sake of spreading the glory of this monumental human achievement.

Seeing the intensity in his Corporate Buddy's eyes, and more out of a sense of safety than interest, Kai takes the remaining two jelly beans and places them on his tongue carefully, like a communion wafer in a Catholic church.

His first sensation is the taste of artificial fruit of some kind, followed by the additional flavor and texture of cheap coffee powder. Then, as the different composites of beans begin to combine into a kind of thick soup on his palate, there is an unidentifiable taste that reminds him of something that might be dug up from the bottom of a muddy river in an uninhabited location, followed by a dim reminiscence of the artificial butter that would go on popcorn: but not actually the taste of popcorn.

With his host glaring silently and expectantly at his expression (like NASA engineers in the control room waiting to find out that the space unit did, in fact, touch down upon the moon), Kai licks his tongue around his teeth (there is an unpleasant, waxy, plastic-like coating upon them all of a sudden, which has layered upon the sensation produced earlier by Wendy's homemade cookies).

The Euro-expat then makes the diplomatic and variously interpretable statement of "Amazing", to which Big Jim extends himself a bit taller and nods his head up and down, in agreement of how absolutely incredible this technology and, thereby, America as a whole actually is.

"Pretty impressive stuff, ain't it?", Jim says, with self-assurance of the obvious answer.

The expatriate from Germany is scowling as he licks his teeth.

"Bet ya' never had anything like *that* over there in *Europe*!", Jim states proudly, sure that the wonders of the visitor's new homeland have now begun to dawn upon him.

Meanwhile, Kai senses a conflict developing in his stomach, which is expanding slowly to take over some of his other, less suspecting organs.

"You should try the Strawberry-Cola-Marmalade", Wendy says, to which her husband adds an affirmative and factual "*De*finitely."

Suddenly, the phone rings sharply. Wendy slaps the "Speaker" button and says, "Hel-LOO-oo?"

"According to our files, your debt is in the *R-R-Red Zone*!", the automated voice of the robocall grumbles deeply, like a monster in a horror movie. "With our new Debt Enhancement program…"

MaxiFoods

At the traffic light, the German expatriate sits and watches the giant, bright-orange inflatable advertisement-man undulate its body parts ominously in front of the "TireWorld!" parking lot.

The figure rages high up into the bright sky, performing a discordant dance to some unheard, insane rhythm in its own head. It looks as if it will reach out at any moment to grab carloads of customers from the roadside and drag them in to have their tires changed or rotated, willingly or otherwise – all at a discount and with a free cup of coffee.

As Kai watches, mesmerized by the unpredictable movements, the inflato-man turns its head slowly and silently in his direction. Then it suddenly arches its upper arm into the air, followed fluidly by its forearm and hand, and then quickly flicks its five wriggly streamer-fingers up into the clouds, as if batting them away.

Then, the figure bends strangely forward at the hips and the arm swoops downwards towards Kai, and the giant hand floats closer and closer. As the flailing streamers extend, Kai's own fingers tighten on the steering wheel. He looks down the road, and then back at the giant inflato-man, which is now closer than before – unpleasantly close.

As the traffic light turns green, Kai pounds his foot into the gas pedal of his two-door hybrid car. A few moments later, he sees the fingers in his rearview mirror flicking like sharpened talons behind him, and he sees the demonic face of the inflated, bright-orange creature raising upwards as it laughs at the sun.

More attentive than before, Kai drives onwards, past the first boxy, rectangular strip mall on the right.

Each colorful, boisterous sign seems to call out "We're a *very* special company with a *one-of-a-kind* personality!", as the signs protrude from their systematic location against the background of the drab, beige wall.

In the strip mall, there is a sign for "Mama Ragata's Italian Restaurant", promising a moment of luxurious exotic dining with a Mediterranean flair, right in between "H&L Shoes" on one side and "Payday Loans" on the other. On the wall, behind the sign for the loan shop, there is the faded mark of a "Bridal Boutique" sign that has since come and gone.

After the strip mall, there is a used-car shop, with multi-colored streamers fluttering sharply in the roadside wind. High above the entrance to the building is an American flag, its colors faded from the sun and its edges jagged and tattered from wear.

Next to it is a store with a sign that just says "Guns n' Beer".

Driving on, Kai passes under a huge billboard that rages out from the sand and weeds near the sidewalk. It shows a statue holding a scale in one hand, with its other hand raised in a clenched fist. "Bransky Legal Firm", the billboard states. "You have RIGHTS. Get what's YOURS!".

A few minutes later, Kai turns left at the towering "MaxiFoods" sign. After the tight parking lot entrances and spaces overseas, there is a sense of luxury as he drives onto the wide expanse of perfectly even, light-gray macadam.

The supermarket parking lot is larger than the popular European beach where he spent his vacation last year. If it weren't for the cars in front of the building, a small plane could easily land there.

Kai enjoys the ample room to drive and maneuver. There is not the sense that he has to function with pinpoint accuracy so as to avoid bumping into the other vehicles, like back home. It's like there is a bubble of comfort and leisure around his car, and there is a sense of ease and relief at not having to concentrate so much as he turns down one of the gaping lanes to find a place to park.

As he does so, the brown car driving in front of him passes an empty space and continues on closer to the store, where it sits and waits for a customer to get into a car and vacate the closer space.

Kai chooses the first space at the end of the mass of vehicles. As he pulls in, his car is dwarfed by a wall of SUVs to the left, right and front of him. It is as if a set of towering skyscrapers have just blocked out the sun.

He opens his door cautiously, like back home, so as not to bang into the neighboring vehicle, and then he is reminded of how much room there is between the cars in American parking lots. He sees someone in the next lane swing open a car door wide and free, without care or concern, as if the door has suddenly been released by a spring. As Kai gets out, he sees that he will not be needing to fold in his side view mirror to make more space, like he often has to do in Germany.

The rest of the parking lot is also filled with one mammoth sports utility vehicle after another: hulky, dark machines, lined up like a fleet of tanks ready to go to war. Together, they look like the Holocaust monument in Berlin, with its row upon row of tall, stone slabs surrounding their deep, lonely alleys and intersections.

Far away in a corner of the parking lot, away from the other vehicles, there is a conglomeration of cars and vans, all parked in different directions, like in a caravan in the old west. They seem as though they are in another universe: a couple of the vans have awnings extended, and people are sitting in lawn chairs amongst the cars, chatting as they eat out of bags and plastic containers, like at a dysfunctional picnic.

Kai has heard of these parking lot settlements; they are people who sometimes describe themselves as being "on the road", but who in fact are living out of their cars and vans because they cannot afford an apartment. Some have been thrown out of the homes that they bought in the lead-up to the 2008 financial crisis, after they could no longer afford the mortgages that were higher than their houses turned out to be worth after the crash. Some of the people drive from the parking lot to their office jobs every morning, only to return to their unofficial space outside Maxi-Foods at night, and some were simply downsized in a corporate process that is euphemistically known as "creative destruction". Some gave up in their late fifties and just accepted being forced into "early retirement" – and some are just hanging on, day by day.

The Euro-expat sighs and turns to walk the few yards to the store (though he still thinks of it as a few meters, having grown up with the metric system. "Groups of ten", he often says to people. "It is so eassy and makes so much sense").

He has to walk around the discarded shopping carts that are scattered here and there. He finds it strange that the Americans run the risk of their expensive vehicles being smashed into and scratched by an unattended shopping cart.

Back home, the carts each have a slot for a chip that the customer inserts to free the cart from the little chain that holds it in place. After shopping, the customer returns the cart to one of the collection points, reinserts the chain, his chip pops out, and he takes it with him to his safe, scratchless automobile.

However, with this other system here, the Americans *do* save themselves the effort of having to walk back to return the shopping carts, which is good because… because they would otherwise be in danger of unnecessarily burning too many calories.

If that happened, they might starve, right there in the supermarket parking lot – unless, of course, they were to bring a bag of chips along with them for sustenance, until they reach the safety of their cars again.

In the parking lot, Kai comes upon a young man in a shirt that matches the colors of the MaxiFoods sign and who is rushing about collecting the carts.

"Hi!", the worker shouts out as he smiles to the customer walking next to him. His voice is cordial, but tight, and high – as if he is under pressure to collect all of the carts as quickly and efficiently as possible, warmly greet all of the customers he passes who are "enjoying their shopping experience at MaxiFoods", and to look gleeful while doing so.

On the young man's nametag, Kai reads "Hi! I'm Brad, your Parking Lot Engineer!"

At the end of the parking lot near the storefront, Kai walks past the same brown car that had been in front of him when he entered the lane. The driver of the car is still in the difficult process of excavating himself from the driver's seat, heaving his weight by pulling with both hands on the upper frame of the car. The driver sticks one leg out, and then the next, and little by little, he wiggles himself free. It looks like a big baby chicken hatching from an egg – an egg equipped with four-wheel drive and surround sound speakers.

In front of the store, Kai takes a shopping cart from the row, and he feels again a sense of ease and convenience at the simple release of the cart, without having to unlink the little chain like back home.

The cart is gigantic – not simply as large as the bigger shopping carts found in the discount stores in Europe today: America outgrew those little playthings around the end of the 1980's. These shopping carts are rolling monuments, each large enough to carry a malnourished family of seven Guatemalan immigrants across the border.

There is also a certain comfort that these carts provide; in the event that this particular American town becomes one of the many to be decimated by a natural disaster, the shopping carts are large enough to contain all of one's major earthly possessions.

As Kai enters the store, the giant glass door *wooshes* open for him, and he instantly walks into a thick wall of cold air from the air conditioner, like in his office. In fact, as he crosses the threshold, the front half of him is already pleasantly cooled, while the back half of him still feels the heat from the wilds of the uncivilized world outside. The sensation enhances the feeling that there must be something wonderful about shopping here.

He is instantly in a jungle of brightly colored fruits and leafy green vegetables of all kinds. There is a sense of fullness and abundance, as if he is in a highly-fertile rain forest. There might just as well be colorful parrots flying amongst the ventilation ducts and a toucan squatting by the pineapples.

In the produce displays, there is one long, perfectly stacked pyramid after another, and in spite of all the shopping, there is somehow never a single piece of fruit or any other item missing (since any removed product is always immediately replaced with another of its kind, before any sense of absence or a lack of plentitude can be noticed).

There is also not the occasional grey-black, rotting orange or mango among the others, with all of them still for sale, like in Europe.

As Kai looks at the fruit, he sees that they are all shining brightly, like emeralds that have recently been polished. There is no waxy appearance to the skins of the apples, and they are all gigantic and perfectly shaped.

Everything looks just *fantastic!*

… but still, nothing looks real, exactly.

The fruit all looks like it wasn't grown, per se, as much as it was fabricated; as if it was manufactured, marketed, and displayed for the customer's convenience, but as though the entire process had nothing whatsoever to do with such filthy inconveniences and inconsistencies as sunlight, earth and seasonal cycles.

Kai looks at a pile of pale strawberries, each of them the size of a child's hand.

Then, he remembers the bowl of plastic fruit and artificial flowers from the breakfast bar at Big Jim's and Wendy's house, and for a moment, he is not sure if what he is looking at is actual produce.

'Is this where they get the pretend fruit for their centerpieces?', he wonders.

He looks closer at the fruit, to inspect it. In the surface of the polished apples, he sees dozens of reflections of his own face, frowning.

Looking from one glorious pile to the next, he cannot find anything that stimulates his appetite.

'There is certainly a lot, but none of it looks like it has any taste'', he says to himself.

'Don't they *like* fruit?', he thinks (he doesn't have an accent when he thinks to himself – in his own German mind, he speaks English perfectly).

He takes a few pears, which are so hard that they could be used like rocks in a violent street protest. After adding a few vegetables and some other produce, he continues on.

The aisles are as wide and inviting as the lanes in the parking lots. There is enough space for Kai's oversized shopping cart to pass the others without any concern, while still leaving plenty of room for him to be able to perform a tango down the middle of the aisle – if he were that sort of person.

'There is certainly no lack of space in America', Kai says to himself.

Then, he remembers how close Big Jim's house was to that of his neighbor.

'In public, anyhow', he adds.

He also notices that the stores are so much more organized than the ones in Europe: everything has its place, and everything is easily accessible. There are not three different sections of nuts scattered all over the store, so that a person has to hunt for them like a wild animal foraging in the woods. There's just "the nut section" (adorned with promotional material that says "Let's go *NUTS!!*", next to the cartoon of a bug-eyed beaver with buck teeth biting into a walnut).

The European shopper also notices that there are also no advertising displays blocking him from moving in the aisles and reaching the products that he wants to buy. They displays are all on the perpendicular ends of the aisles, like a little surprise distraction as he turns the corner, and as if he is being offered something extra, something special – not something that he can stumble over and break his leg.

The signs are also like little playthings, almost toys. Above a display of flavored lemonade packs at the tip of one aisle, for example, there is a wooden sign hung from a string and, of course, a bushel of fresh lemons to stimulate the imagination. It is as if the lemons have been freshly plucked in a small town, squeezed into these self-standing juice packs, mixed with preservatives and artificial cherry flavor, and placed here for sale. The wooden sign says "*Cool!!*" in bright blue casual script, as though some dear friend (from the distribution department of the international foods conglomerate) just happened to come by and scrawl it there himself, for Kai to enjoy.

These shop displays are each like a little movie. There's some story behind them. They're entertaining.

As he passes the tremendous array of products that fill the shelves to bursting, Kai has the impression that American supermarkets are truly a monument to efficiency and salesmanship.

At the same time, he is aware of a sharp contrast between how well *presented* everything is, and how *good* everything actually seems to be.

He turns down one aisle and sees a party-colored wall of every – possible – variety of sugary breakfast cereal that humans on the earth can possibly imagine, concoct and distribute. There are boxes with cartoons of pop-eyed frogs, pop-eyed chickens, pop-eyed monsters – all apparently popping their eyes due to the high sugar content of the products that they are promoting.

And the cereal boxes are all thick and gigantic – Kai watches a woman take a box of "Krispy Donut Rings" from the shelf, and her hand can barely wrap around it as she lifts it and places it in the cart, where her unsuspecting, pudgy-cheeked offspring reaches its two hands out to receive it.

'They have a thousand kinds of breakfast cereal, but only one variety of pears', Kai says to himself.

Throughout the store, in nearly every category of prepared item, there is a well-spring of "low-fat" products for sale: low fat cookies, low-fat crackers, low fat yogurt, even low-fat butter.

'When they take out the fat, what do they put back in its place?', Kai wonders.

As he reaches out for a box of dry crackers, there is a severely overweight woman down the aisle putting one box of "Low-fat Caramel Wafers" after another into her cart. From the mass of her hips and the thickness of her wrists, it is evident that the wafers aren't working.

'Low-fat caramel', the European engineer wonders to himself. 'How can they do that?'

In the next aisle, he is standing before an assortment of "Pork Rinds", wondering how many different flavors of fried pig fat there can actually be, when he is surprised by a sudden high-pitched scream from behind him.

For a moment, he imagines one of the pigs squealing, and then he distinguished his name, "KA-ai!!".

He turns around to see Wendy, Jim's wife.

"Oh, hallo, Vendy. It is good to see you."

She is clutching an over-sized bag of "Low-Carb Party Chips!" in both hands.

'Big Jim', Kai guesses.

"It's so *great* to *SEE* you he-e-e-er!", Wendy says, and then she stands there and smiles at him without saying anything else, as if being smiled at is sufficiently wonderful.

She sees him looking at the giant bag of chips and she says, "Oh", as if the story behind the chips is just terribly frustrating, "They're for Jim."

"I see", Kai says.

"Yea. He likes the regular kind, but the doctor told him…" (and she puts one hand on her hip and shakes her other index finger at the space next to Kai, as if imagining someone is there) "either you cut down on the *cholesterol* or you won't live to see any *grandkids*!".

Then, she breaks character and laughs hysterically at her own rendition.

Kai is taken aback at the intimacy of this detail of her and her husband's private life that she has just "shared" with him.

"Zat must be serious," Kai says evenly, trying to respond politely while still trying to maintain what he considers to be a suitable personal distance.

"Oh, *you* know how he is", she says, frowning and smiling at the same time as she waves a hand in the air.

"I do?"

Kai accidentally said this one out loud, and after Wendy's initial look of shock and confusion at the response, she resorts to what makes her feel safe: hysterical laughter.

As she howls, her gums are exposed, and Kai is surprised at how pink they are.

At the end of her fit, she gasps for breath, slaps her upper thigh and releases a slow, descending "OOH-h-h-h-h-h-h", as if to say "THAT was a good one!".

Then, putting into words what she managed to come up with during her attack, she says to the European expatriate, "You must be over*whelmed* with all this good food, Kai."

Kai looks around at the snack shelves, and he notices that there is an entire subsection filled with different kinds and colors of "Salsa!".

"Zer is a lot to chooss from", he says, keeping his thoughts to himself.

"Oh, I know", Wendy says, as if they are comrades who share a common understanding, "We heard that they stand on long lines in Europe to get bread, and that the shelves are empty."

Kai is taken aback. An image of the wall of cold-cuts and imported European cheeses from his local supermarket back in Germany flashes before his eyes.

'She thinks the war is still on', he realizes.

Then he notices that she said "we".

'Do they all think the war is still on?', he wonders, as he looks at her a bit studiously.

"Well, welcome to the land of great food!", Wendy shouts as she throws her arms up into the air and smiles exuberantly at Kai, as if saying to a child, "You just won the *BIG PRIZE*!".

"Sank, you, Vendy. Dat is very kind of you."

She lowers her arms suddenly to her sides and smiles as she looks back at him; she is used to getting more of a reaction for her performances than this.

"Well, anyway", she finally says, realizing that this was the sum total of Kai's reaction, "I gotta go", and she throws her thumb over her shoulder, as if she's hitch-hiking backwards. She starts to laugh again, and then tries to stifle it. "Gotta pick up Bart from rifle practice… *GREAT* seeing ya, Kai. Ya *GOTTA* come by again sometime!"

"OK, I vill do dat", Kai says, accepting the offer (he doesn't realize that this is just something Americans say to be polite and to carry the conversation along, and that they don't really mean it. He also doesn't know that when he goes to visit them a couple of days later to take them up on their invitation, Jim will answer the door in his boxer shorts and a soiled tank top, scratching his belly and cradling the big bag of "Low-Carb Party Chips!" in his arm, and that Wendy will be sitting on the sofa in her pajamas watching TV).

"OK. Bye bye, Kai – Oh! Bye bye – Kai!", and she twitters at the rhyme she thinks she has just been the first to stumble upon.

"Bye bye, Vendy", Kai says, as he waves to her from the snack aisle.

As she goes, turning back around to wave several times, he looks at her cart: it is filled to overflowing with "Shug-a-Flakes!" and other breakfast cereals, two of the giant bags of chips, a similar one of tortilla chips, towering piles of plastic containers filled with meat, as well as canned goods and packages with the words "Ready-to-Eat!" on them.

He turns around to his own cart with the pears, vegetables and crackers in it. It looks like a starter cart compared to what he has just seen.

From the other end of the aisle comes a shiny-red motorized vehicle at a peculiarly slow speed. There is a man sitting in it; he is about 30 years old and severely obese. As he pulls up to the shelf, he reaches with difficulty to grasp one of the giant bags of "Toasty Fries!" and then he tosses it into the wagon area of the motorized vehicle.

As a second such vehicle starts to come from around the corner, Kai turns swiftly and heads out the other way, towards the checkout.

When he gets there, he is relieved that Wendy is not still on line.

As he waits, he sees the sign above the aisle next to him. "Express. 10 Items or Less", it says, and he sees people with a few items in their carts going through at a comparatively rapid speed.

'What a great idea!', he thinks.

Back home, there is no such option, and people with only a few items to buy either happen to come across a friendly soul in front of them who lets them go ahead, or they just wait, quietly, and bear it.

He sees the man in the red motorized vehicle slide in behind him, so he decides to just stay where he is.

The cashier is covered with several company pins and tags on her chest, and she is wearing a hat with another pin on it that says "MaxiFoods Loves *YOU*!"

After the cashier offers a "Thank you for having a great day with me at Maxi Foods!" to the lady in line before him, the cashier turns to Kai and says, "Hi! Did you find everything you were looking for today at MaxiFoods?"

The European is a bit taken aback by the question. Then, he pauses, and he thinks of all the items he was used to from back home that he wanted to get today and couldn't find, like a certain kind of soft French cheese that he likes, thinly sliced prosciutto, his dark chocolate, and…

53

He decides not to go into the matter, and he says, "It vas fine, sank you", and he smiles politely to the cashier, who looks up at him when she notices his accent.

There is a teenage boy at the end of the counter who begins to stick Kai's goods into a plastic bag with remarkable speed and agility. The plastic bag is held open by a metal structure, and its mouth looks like the open mouth of a shark that has been caught and strung up on a pier.

Kai reaches for the onions and says, "Oh, I can do zat", and he pulls out the cloth bags that he had brought in with him and starts to bag the groceries himself, like back home.

"That's OK", the teenager says, "I'll take care of that for you, sir", and the boy smiles to Kai while taking the onions and putting them in the bag, as if there is no question about the matter.

Kai is pleasantly surprised at both the service and the friendliness he is receiving, but he is a bit flustered by the fact that he has not been asked if he even wants to receive this service – that it has rather been imposed upon him.

"OK, but I vould radder use my own cloth bags, if you do not mind, sir", Kai says, holding up the bags that he had brought in with him.

Without a pause in his strategic movements, the bagger, who is also covered with an array of pins and tags, says, "Sorry, sir, we have to use plastic or paper."

Kai is at a loss as to what to do, and how to get the teenager to stop or even slow down his movements and how to convince him of the benefits of cloth bags instead of plastic ones, which are bad for the environment.

"Well, dees are my own bags, you see", Kai offers as a solution.

"Sorry, sir. We are not permitted to use outside conveyances. It's for hygienic reasons, sir."

Kai is a little insulted that this mere boy has just questioned the man's cleanliness and domestic habits, but he quickly realizes that it is company policy and not a decision that the boy has made himself. After wondering what the reason for such a decision could be, Kai remembers the billboard that he saw on his way to the supermarket, and he assumes that the company is worried that it could be sued.

"I cannot use my own bags?", the customer says.

"Sorry, sir. It's for your own well-being".

The European man folds up his cloth bags neatly and holds them close to his abdomen.

"Sank you", Kai says sarcastically, to which the bagger responds, "It's my pleasure, sir!", with a big smile on his face and a warm, attentive gaze as he continues his hectic movements.

The cashier takes the opportunity during this break in the conversation to ask Kai, "Where ya from, it ya don't mind me askin', sir?".

Kai turns to her, surprised again by the informality, as well as the request for such personal details about his life by the person ringing up his groceries.

Back home, it is not long ago that they strengthened the data protection regulations about how companies handle their customers' information.

She seems like she is legitimately curious, so he says, "I am from Chermany."

The woman smiles and inhales a stream of air from her suddenly parting lips.

"No kiddin!", she says, staring with wonder and cordiality at the German customer. "*I'M* German!"

"Really?", Kai says, not imagining that this could be true. She just *looks* so American.

Then, as she continues to pass the items across the scanner, she rolls her eyes up playfully, and says, "Welp", as if about to start on a long explanation of the matter of her heritage, and adds, "my great-*grand*parents came from Germany, a long time ago", and she shakes her head very, very fast back and forth, as if it is so long ago that it can't be remembered anymore.

"Hey, my last name used to be Altgeschwür…", then she looks up and to the side, flicks her hand back at the wrist, and says, "that is, before my grandfather changed it. What does it mean, anyway?", she asks him, scowling now at the serious and insightful question.

Kai doesn't have the heart to tell her that her family's former name means "old festering sore", so he says, "I am not sure. It might be from dialect".

Then the cashier looks upwards and to the side again and says, "Oh… COOL!!", as if she has made a decision, and then rings up the total.

Kai handles the bill, and the friendly cashier smiles warmly to him and says "Have fun in America… and thank you for having a great day with me at Maxi Foods!"

Kai looks at her.

"Sank you. I vill... I mean, I did, I... sank you."

And the cashier smiles further to him before turning to the man in the red motorized wheelchair and saying to him "Hi! Did you find everything you were looking for today at MaxiFoods?"

As the bagger puts the second bag next to the first in Kai's shopping cart, Kai thanks him and goes to leave, when he suddenly feels the cart lurch a bit.

It's an old man, but he is dressed in exactly the same uniform as the boy who bagged Kai's groceries, and the man is covered with the same pins and tags.

"I'll take that cart out for you today, sir!". The elderly man says it as if he has just thought of this great idea, and decided to help out a bit.

"Hum? Oh, no, dat is OK, I can take it myself". Kai responds.

"That's OK, sir, I'll be *glad* to take your cart out to your vehicle for you!"

At the mention of the official word "vehicle" instead of the more common "car", Kai realizes that he is up against some more inflexible corporate policy, which is all for his own good.

At the same time, Kai finds it inappropriate that he, a young man, has an elderly man offering to carry his groceries for him. 'It should be the other way around', the expatriate thinks. 'I should be helping *him*.'

"But... it is on wheels", Kai reasons.

"That's OK, sir, I can take your cart out to your vehicle for you!", the old man repeats.

There is a look in the worker's eyes and face, as if to say, "Please, don't make this difficult. They're watching", and Kai realizes that the man is required to take the cart out to the car, that this is his job, and that the man apparently needs the money. Otherwise, he would be retired already, and be at home with his family, or playing cards with his friends, or… something, anything other than this.

"OK", Kai says, and he lets the elderly man push his cart out to his car for him, even though he feels a bit guilty in the process.

In the parking lot, Kai sees other customers walking out behind workers who are pushing their carts for them. Some of the workers are teenagers, but another one is a man who is also clearly over the normal retirement age.

There is also a young teenager, a "Parking Lot Engineer", collecting the loose and straying shopping carts from around the lot.

'Maybe it's a way to prevent so many carts from having to be collected later', Kai thinks to himself.

As he walks, he watches the old man in front of him, hunched over the cart – his scrawny, furry arms bent and poking out to the sides – and Kai thinks of Zackary, the contract worker at his office, and wonders if this is what will become of him.

Kai has to hold himself back as he watches the elderly man strain to lift the bags and put them in the trunk of the car.

After Kai offers his thanks, the man stands there a bit longer than necessary and says, "OK, thank you, sir. Have a good day. And thank you for shopping at MaxiFoods," and then smiles before turning to head back to the store.

Kai doesn't know that although it is not required, some customers give the man a dollar as a tip, mostly out of commiseration, and because they understand. The teenagers sometimes get some spare change.

As Kai closes his trunk, he is surprised by a passing "Hayadoon" spoken to him by a chubby, tattooed man in a tank top. The man has severe sun-burn and is carrying a can of shaving cream, a bar of soap and a bag of chips in his hands and is heading to the settlement of cars and vans that is gathered in the far corner of the parking lot. He looks friendly, but Kai can see deep bags beneath the man's eyes, as if he has been up late at night (perhaps figuring a way out of his predicament, fighting with his wife about the way out… who knows).

From inside his car, Kai watches the man as he reaches the conglomeration of vehicles in the corner. He is greeted tiredly by the people who are sitting outside in their folding chairs, in the shade of the giant billboard that towers above them from the roadside at their backs.

On the billboard, there is a picture of a man in a suit and tie, and he's holding a fist full of cash.

"Invest online and get RICH, like ME!", the words of the billboard shout.

There is a thick, sapphire ring on one of the fingers that is wrapped around the cash.

All the Rage

Big Jim's younger brother, Alex, is just settling himself and his two children into their seats in the airplane. After a contentious battle, he got visiting rights for the week from his ex-wife and is taking them along to visit their uncle.

"Family!", he shouts gruffly at his daughter as he tugs the seat belt a little too tightly into place at her lap. "*SOME* people, like your *mother*, don't think it's so important."

And then he places his hands tightly on the upper arms of his young son, shakes him into place, and straps him in. The daughter watches this and then starts to suck on the new "Sugar Ring" that she's wearing around her finger. Seeing this, her younger brother starts to lick the one on his finger, as well. Hers is cherry, and his is raspberry.

"The *last* thing I needed today was that *jerk* at the cigarette stand in the airport", Alex blurts. Then, he flops down into his own seat with a loud "*Plump!*", shaking the two children in their seats next to him as they take refuge in their candies.

He turns to the seat between his and his daughter.

"He didn't have to ask you if you want one too!", he shouts at his son, as if the six-year-old is to blame for the events that transpired. "I already *told* him I wanted two Sugar Rings!"

Alex shakes his head as he stews in his sense of violated justice.

"That guy *deserved* to be told what an *idiot* he was. There was no reason for him to call security like that."

There is silence as the children vacantly look straight ahead and continue sucking on their candy rings.

"With *kids* there!", Alex adds angrily. "Man! Doesn't *anybody* have and re*SPECT* anymore?!"

Already this weekend, when he picked the children up from their maternal grandparents' house, there was an argument about the well-being of the children – which is what he told the police the reason for his "road rage" was, after he was pulled over for screaming through the passenger-side window over the head of his daughter at a driver that was going too slow, and then swerving back and forth in front of the other car after he overtook it.

"How could *I* know that it was a cop in an unmarked car?", he yelled to his daughter after he threw the ticket in her lap and sped off with them in the car.

Then there was that heated argument with the barista in the coffee shop about… whatever it was.

Alex has been on behavior-altering medication for about as long as anyone can remember; he started with Ritalin when he was a child, and the doctors and his parents just kept "upping the ante". There was a sharp increase in the prescriptions after he was court-ordered for anger management a year and a half ago. Now, it's a heady cocktail of medically prescribed Prozac, various opioids and other painkillers, along with a constant incoming dosage of various kinds of alcohol. He describes the last contribution as "part of his own, personal medical plan".

His daughter started on Ritalin a few months ago. The school psychologist said that she appeared "nervous", and the girl's fourth-grade teacher complained that the child was "just always fidgeting around". There are discussions about the son starting on a similar medication after he returns from this trip.

At this early stage, his children are already well on their way to following in their father's footsteps – much like the Rothschild or Napoleon dynasties, but in an entirely different way.

As the plane starts rolling forward on the tarmac, a pair of little, beady eyes pops up from the seat in front of the man. His children laugh, and it turns out to be a squirrel.

"What'r *you* starin' at?!", the father says defiantly to the little, dark-eyed animal.

The man in the seat in front turns around and says, "Oh, I'm sorry, that's Benny. He's my emotional-support animal."

"What?", Alex says to the man.

"Yea, I get a little nervous on flights, and my psychiatrist told me that I should just take Benny along, for a little help."

Alex turns to his two children, with a look that says, 'See? I *told* you so!'.

The daughter raises her eyes to her father, with her head bent deeply over her Sugar Ring. The boy is still just licking and staring straight ahead at the back of the seat in front of him – they're expecting turbulence.

Then their father turns to the man in the row in front of him and shouts, "I never heard of anything so stupid in all my life!". He says it as if it is a judicial declaration, and that the matter is now settled irrevocably.

62

"Don't call Benny stupid!", the other man says, putting his finger tips near where the squirrel's ears are, as if to protect it from hearing the insult. The little animal just chirps and starts to chew on the plastic curve of the seat back.

"OK", Alex says, as if taking up a challenge, "how 'bout I just call *you* stupid, you stupid jerk?! An emotional-support squirrel. Did you ever hear of such a thing?". This time, he calls it out into the plane fuselage, assuming the support of some angry, likewise offended mass behind him.

The man's gentle eyes turn sharper, and then they soften again as he sniffs the air, finding in it a means of defense.

"Maybe you shouldn't drink so early, sir", he says, as he turns around and exchanges a glance with a woman across the aisle from him. They both raise their eyebrows to each other.

"Oh yea? Maybe *you* shouldn't be a *jerk-off* so early! How 'bout *THAT*?!", and he nods his head down and up once, quickly, in affirmative defiance.

The man doesn't respond.

After Alex sees that there will be no further shots fired, he lets out a "Man!", shakes his head back and forth, and looks vacantly at the seat back with his eyebrows smashing into each other.

Then, "Boop!" – the little squirrel's face suddenly pops up in front of him again. The furry animal turns his face to the children and wiggles its nose, and they start to giggle, with their heads still bent cautiously over their Sugar Rings.

With the giggling, Alex feels his grasp slipping – his grasp on the argument, his grasp on his family, and (most important of all) his grasp on justice, as he perceives it.

"Oh, that's it!", he shouts, and then he bangs with his two clenched fists on the curved plastic top of the seat back, just missing the agile squirrel.

The frightened emotional-support animal scurries onto the head of his owner and starts screeching, dancing around and around on the man's balding head and pulling the remaining thin hairs up into a tuft around himself.

"Benny!", the man underneath the frightened squirrel calls, with his own eyes raised up into his forehead to try and see his little friend. And then he adds, "Don't worry, he can't hurt you", trying to reason with the creature.

"Oh, you don't think so?", Alex grumbles. "Just be glad I don't hurt *you*, you *jerk-off*!"

Meanwhile, the plane has rolled slowly to a standstill. A stewardess in a little blue hat rushes over, adorns her face with a warm smile, and greets the little squirrel that is still atop the balding man's head. Amongst all the ruckus, the animal has built a little nest for itself from among the thin, dry strands.

Then, the stewardess' smile melts away as she turns to the loud man in row 32, one seat in from the end.

Replacing her current stern expression with another, more officious smile from among her collection, she informs Alex, "I'm sorry, sir, but we'll have to ask you and your children to exit the aircraft."

She turns to the children and bends her own head to one side. This time, she has chosen a smile of sorrowful empathy.

"WHAT?!", Alex blurts out at the slender young woman in the smart, blue dress. "You're not seriously gonna take *their* side?!", referring to his current arch enemies: the balding, fragile man and his nervous, emotional-support squirrel.

"Sir, please", the stewardess says, bent at the waist with her hands folded before her.

"That guy's a *PSYCHO!*", Alex erupts, as if it would be ridiculous to not notice that fact. "You actually wanna take the side of a crazy *psycho* and that filthy *varmint* over a *real AMERICAN*?!"

The stewardess looks at him attentively for one moment further, and then hurries away.

"Hmm!", Alex says, turning to his timid children, as if they are supposed to have learned something from the event.

"See? Not *everybody's* a fragile pushover", he tells them.

Then, he turns forward and shouts at the plastic seat-back in front of him. "You hear that, *SQUIRRLY BOY?!!*", and then he gives the seat back an added little punch from behind, making it shake.

Upon the sound of contact, the boy bites abruptly into his raspberry Sugar Ring, and there is only a broken chunk of candy left on the plastic yellow ring around his finger.

Reveling in his sense of victory, although not being able to enjoy it due to his anger, Alex sits back and pouts as he stews in his aisle seat.

After a few minutes, as he's fumbling around with the latch for the dinner tray in front of him, the security guard from the cigarette stand event enters the plane, and exchanges a few words with the stewardess, who extends a slender finger down the aisle towards where Alex is sitting.

"Oh, no. Not *this* clown again!", he says.

As the security guard steps further into the aircraft, another security guard appears behind him and follows. This one is bigger than the first one.

Alex looks straight ahead, in the hopes that they will not see him.

As they appear above him at his side, the smaller of the two security guards, who is in the front, say, "Excuse me, sir, but you and your children will have to vacate the aircraft."

Alex looks up, sizes up the two security guards, and then chortles out a little laugh as he says, "You're not serious?!"

He's hoping that he can talk them out of it and that the two security guards will eventually just go away.

"Please collect any carry-on baggage and vacate the aircraft… sir", the same security guard says.

The two guards are standing more rigidly now.

Alex is aware that the second, larger security guard has not yet spoken. The man looks alert, though… ready.

"I'm on my way to bring my kids to see their uncle", Alex complains. "I can't just *leave*."

"Please, sir" the first security guard says.

"But the squirrel *started* it!", Alex bursts out, as if everything else he has been hearing is entirely beyond reason. "He was *staring me down*! Right, kids?!"

As he turns to his children for support, he sees that they are just staring quietly up at the two security guards in the aisle, as if hypnotized.

"If you don't go now, sir, you'll have to be removed", the first security guard says.

"This whole thing is so *stupid*!", Alex shouts, throwing his hands up into the air of the fuselage. "This country is falling *apart*!".

From behind, the bigger security guard now states, calmly and coolly, "If you don't vacate the area, you will be removed", as his partner looks at the man's children.

The large man's hand is resting alertly upon some sort of short, black baton.

"Oh, this is such *crap*!, Alex says, banging at the air with his clenched fists.

"*COME* on, kids", he shouts, as the children wince at the sudden attention, "Let's get outta here.. before they put your father in *prison* because he stood *up* for his *RIGHTS*!".

There's a lot of banging and rummaging around as Alex unstraps his children and drags them out into the aisle. It's a far more boisterous procedure than it needs to be.

As he steps next to the security guards to get his carry-on bag from the compartment overhead, he notices that the second security guard is considerably taller and larger than he is. The first security guard places his palm out and cups it next to the children's heads, to prevent them from getting knocked against the hard plastic of the seat-back.

Alex rips open the hatch of the overhead compartment and rummages around like a frenzied animal for his carry-on baggage.

"I don't know how I'm gonna get these kids to see their uncle now", he grumbles into the compartment, as if the entire tragedy as well as any further psychological damage that might result from it is entirely the fault of the security guards (he has forgotten about the balding man and the squirrel for the moment).

As he walks down the aisle towards the exit, with his children in front and the two security guards in size order behind him, he feels all the eyes of the other passengers on him. Some have their heads down and are peaking up from their open airline magazines, and some are staring directly at what is transpiring.

There are looks of anger, pity, embarrassment and fear, as well as a mixture of these, in various degrees of intensity.

As the combustible entourage passes one of the many people who are filming the event with their phones, Alex shouts to him, "Good!! Record the whole damn thing! I might need to send it to my *lawyer* when I *sue* this *crappy AIRLINE*!"

Alex and his family are escorted off the plane onto the tarmac. He is gesturing at the plane and arguing with the first security guard.

As they look up at the airplane windows, a face with ruffled hair can be seen peering out from the section where they were sitting. It is the man from the seat in front of theirs, and he is lifting the little arm of his emotional-support squirrel up and down, waving goodbye.

The children start to smile and wave back to the squirrel, and the father turns to them with a stern look of fury.

Then he turns to the security guards and says, "You see? What a *psycho* that guy is?!"

The Barbeque

It's another beautiful Saturday afternoon, and Kai Regenbogen, the European expatriate, has been invited to the home of his "Company Buddy", Big Jim, for a barbeque.

"Just family and a few close friends", Jim said. They have barely known each other for more than a couple of weeks; the month before, Kai had been living in an entirely different country – and Jim would still have some degree of trouble pinpointing that country on the map.

As Kai pulls up to the curb in front of Jim's house, he shuts off the purring motor of his mid-sized hybrid and can suddenly hear a tumult of noise and energy spilling out from behind the fence to the backyard. He realizes that whatever awaits him today, it will happen there, within that enclosure.

In front of him, there is already another car (yet another SUV, of course) parked on the other side of the driveway along the curb. It is a young man and a woman; the man clicks his electronic key, and after a "chirp!", he throws open the hatch up into the air.

Kai can see an intricate conglomeration of objects and devices inside the hatchback. The man reaches into the undefined mass and takes out a flat structure, which he pulls at, unfolds, flips around, extends, clicks into place, and sets on the ground before him in the form of an oversized baby carriage. It offers seating for two, and looks like the baby version of the gigantic automobile from which it has recently hatched.

The man then reaches back into the mass of plastic, metal and cloth and retrieves a pale blue carrying bag with a strap, to which he bows as he drapes the strap over his balding head, like an army hero being adorned by a president with the medal of honor. There are little bunnies hopping in a circle on the front of the bag.

Then, there is a form-molded piece of red plastic, with a set of yellow handlebars and three chunky black wheels stuck on it, which the father heaves out from the pile and sets on the grass between the SUV and the sidewalk.

This is followed by another bag (with a picture of spacemen shooting at each other), which he drapes over his head like before, positioning the bunny-bag to the left of his protruding stomach and the space-wars bag to the right. The straps are tight now, due to his stomach holding the two bags firmly apart from each other.

Then, there is his navy-blue fanny pack, which he lifts at the end with one hand as it dangles, like a boa constrictor, before he wraps it around his generous waist and clicks the plastic buckle into place. From his pocket, he removes a hip-holster for his phone, and he slips the clasp of the holster onto his straining, brown belt. Adorned as he is, the father looks as if he is about to enter into a baby war, or perhaps a war against all other babies.

As the man is about to lower the hatch, Kai can hear through the closed windows of his hybrid the muffled, strained voice of the woman who is bent over at the side opening of the SUV.

"Don't forget the baby's milk bottles!", she calls from inside, as if it is not the first time she has said it.

"I didn't!", he responds, rather gruffly, and he lifts the hatch open again and reaches back into the depths of the gaping hole to retrieve a third bag (an insulated model) with the bright yellow words "It's BABY Time!!" curved like a crown atop a cartoon drawing of a scowling baby erupting from the front surface.

This becomes draped over the father's head, too, and, for lack of further space, it lands against the apex of his belly, where it bounces as he hurls the hatch closed and slams it shut, chirping it locked with his electronic key.

"I'm not *finished*!", the wife shouts, still rummaging around in the abdomen of the vehicle.

"Oh", and he chirps the doors to unlock again. "Sorry".

Then, the mother hurls herself erect with effort, and in her arms is a little baby. The mother walks with the child to the back of the SUV and threads the baby's little pink legs into the foot openings of one of the seating areas of the stroller. She fusses around with a couple of settings, extends the little umbrella, rotates the sliding colorful plastic beads in front of the baby for the child to play with, and sticks a rice cake in his mouth, which the child grasps as if by Pavlovian response and starts to gnaw at and drool over.

From the opening that the mother had just vacated, a pair of skinny, little legs and then a pair of pale-pink shorts appear and start climbing down the footrail of the towering vehicle. The girl then hops (down what for her must seem an eternal distance) and lands with a playfully bounce and hop on the grass by the sidewalk. She then runs around to the back and, without any acknowledgement of her father or mother, holds onto the rim of the vacant seating area and stretches her legs up over the side, to finally plop herself into her place in the baby carriage.

She is six years old.

Without a word, as if he is heading out to hoe the crops in the hot sun in the lower forty acres, the father begins the effort of pushing the two children up the inclined driveway. One of the bags is dangling at his side, the other is balanced precariously on the top of his fanny pack and the other is bouncing, bouncing in rhythm against his protruding belly.

The wife is following, draped with various pale-blue and white quilted blankets and carrying her own set of baby toys and plastic distraction devices. The parents both look thoroughly exhausted, as if this is just another leg in their lengthy journey. Meanwhile, the six-year-old girl is bouncing up and down in her seat erratically, as the baby behind her continues to chew and drool.

Realizing that this is as good a time as any, Kai takes a deep breath as he summons his courage, opens the door to his car and steps out.

At the sound of his car door opening and lightly closing shut, the faces of both the father and mother begin to turn into open, gleeful smiles (again, as if by a Pavlovian response) before looking up to see what has made the sound. Then, they see Kai approaching, and they turn to greet him.

"Hello!", the father says, as if he is having just the most fantastic day he could ever dream of. As he extends his hand and shakes Kai's, the space-wars bag slips from atop the fanny pack and falls, tugging its strap tightly around the father's throat. The father winces, but smiles onward, as though focusing through the pain.

"Hallo, I am pleased to meet you", Kai says.

"Oh, you're that man from… where are you from again?", the wife says.

"I am from…"

"ChirpChirp!!"

Kai trembles slightly from the sharp pitch as he looks around him and up into the sky. Realizing that the sound came from the father having locked the SUV with his remote-controlled key during the start of the conversation, the expat resumes, "I am from Chermany".

He is suddenly aware that he is a little tired of having to inform everybody of his heritage, since he doesn't find it to be a particularly important fact that everybody has to know.

"Oh, how *fancy*!", the wife says, tossing her hand in the air and letting it flop back at the wrist, now overflowing with a casual joy that was clearly absent moments ago when extricating herself and her family from the giant vehicle.

"Germany!", the husband says. "Wow!" Then to his children, "Hear that, kids? This man's from *Germany*", as if Kai is a carnival freak in an exhibition.

They continue chatting as they proceed up the driveway. There is a sign on the front door that says "We're in the back. Come on around!", with an arrow pointing sideways and up, to the backyard gate.

As they reach the gate, there is a purchased sign that says "*DANGER! Beware of Dog!*", with the picture of a German Sheppard, snarling with his jaws open. The wording on the sign could just as well say, "Please, don't make us do this to you".

Tacked under the foreboding warning, there is a piece of paper written upon with various colors of magic markers. The craftsy sign includes the jubilant proclamation "We're in Here!", and then, as if an afterthought, the faster scrawl below it of "Come on in!"

Kai reaches to open the gate for the heavily laden father. As the latch clicks and the wooden door swings open, the man is immediately pounced upon by Rock, the black-brown Rottweiler.

Intuitively, Kai steps behind the protective mass of the person in front of him.

The hound snaps its jaws in a loving "Yowp!" just inches from the man's startled face. From his position behind, Kai can smell the foul breath of the animal.

On his back paws, the Rottweiler is just as tall as the father is, and as the muscles of the canine undulate like a boxer in his prime under his shining black-and-brown coat, there is no doubt as to who would be the victor – if a bell ring were to suddenly ring in the beast's head and his impulse were that he go for blood.

Perhaps with only moments remaining, Wendy suddenly rushes to the door, scolds Rock vociferously and sends him away by picking up a rubber chew-ball that she finds on the ground nearby and throwing in somewhere into the belly of the festivities. The Rottweiler releases a tremendous "ROWF!!", leaps on his powerful hind legs in the direction of the ball, and charges headlong and unstoppably after it.

Then, assured that no "situations" are about to occur (like they had with Rock and that unfortunate insurance salesman in the spring), Wendy turns and gets to the business at hand: she suddenly throws her arms open into the air and approaches her newly arrived guests for a big hug – at which Kai again seeks refuge behind the man in front of him.

The women scream at each other with their eyes wide open (similar to what chimpanzees do when they are about to throw their feces at each other. Among the Americans, though, it is a heartfelt and much-appreciated greeting).

As it turns out, they are sisters, and they haven't seen each other since the day before yesterday. That was at the end of a Thursday "Kiddie Carpool", though, and this is a backyard barbeque on a weekend, so it calls for an entirely different expression of freedom and joy.

From behind Wendy, her husband Big Jim walks towards them at the gate, his body leaned back and throwing his feet out in front of himself loosely, like a king strutting leisurely through his court to meet the guests he has been waiting for all along.

Calling out the name of his brother-in-law, he raises his own hand high in the air, opens his fingers wide, and lets his hand soar like a glider to meet that of the other man, landing with the loud sound of meat slapping against meat before they shake hands and exchange a few words of greeting.

Back when his brother-in-law was in financial straits and in danger of declaring bankruptcy, Big Jim put in a good word for him with HR and got him a job in another department in the company. Since then, the man and his family have moved to the area and now live nearby. The two families see each other regularly, and the men have developed a relationship of comfortable leisure.

Jim views this as the best alternative, compared to the arguments with his wife when she tried to pressure him to "just help the poor guy out", screaming shrilly "He's the father of my sister's kids, for Chrisssake!" and his own response that her brother-in-law was a "No-good jackass!".

Now, they talk sports and complain about how politics is hurting their industry, but there is always an unspoken undercurrent that Jim has done him a favor, that they both know it, and that the brother-in-law owes him one.

Then, Jim turns to his European colleague and greets him, and then Kai walks along with him into the heart of the gathering. The host is wearing sandals, and Kai is surprised to see the thick, hairy knuckle of the big toe of the man who normally wears tight black shoes two desks away from him in the office at their strategic defense company.

They arrive at a group of men who are gathered a little ways off from the big beer keg, which itself is protruding from a giant plastic tub of ice under the shady tree in the yard. They are drinking in gulps from the same type of big, red cups that were at Kai's welcoming party at the office a few weeks ago.

"Hey, guys, this is Kai, my 'Company Buddy'", Jim says, throwing an arm around Kai's shoulders.

"HI-I-i-i, Kai-i-i-i", everyone says more or less in unison, as if children greeting the new kid in school at the teacher's request.

"Kai, this is Bill, Nick, Tom...", and they each lean forward when called upon, give Kai a warm look in the eyes and shake his hand, saying, "Hey, Kai", "Hayadoin, man" and "Wassup, dude".

"...and this is my little brother, Alex", Big Jim says, with a tone consisting of family pride, warning and disappointment.

"Hey, Kai. Gladameecha," the brother says.

Pausing at the apparently new vocabulary word, Kai returns the greeting with a fully decipherable "Hello, Alex. It is nice to see you."

After a moment, they all take out their phones, squoosh together and simultaneously take their own version of the same selfie of the group of them. Then, then each step back to the places they were in before, look at their own photo on their own phone, and then show their version of the photo to their friends, who do the same in return. Everybody is satisfied with the result.

There's a brief pause, and the host tries to stir things back up by calling out to the group, "Kai's from Germany!".

He states it proudly, without noticing Kai wincing a little at the comment.

"Yea, I heard about that", one of the guys says. "How was your flight?".

Even though Kai has already been in the country for three weeks, found housing, acquired an automobile and helped protect the country from foreign invaders through his work, the expat nevertheless answers as if he has just come through the turnstiles at the airport.

"It vas fine, sank you."

After another somewhat awkward silence and a few more gulps of beer, the same man turns to Alex and asks, "What about you, Alex. How was *your* flight?"

Big Jim looks at the ground as he shakes his head just perceptibly from side to side, at which Alex looks at his brother, stretches his own eyes wide and shouts to him, "That skinny little varmint didn't even belong on the *PLANE*!"

Big Jim looks his brother firmly in the eye, and Alex shouts out at no one in particular, "I need another beer!". Then, he whirls around impetuously and takes a few big, stomping strides to the other side of the tree where the beer keg is. He fills his cup to the brim (shaking the little black dispenser hose in his hand trying to make the beer come out faster, even though this doesn't change anything), and as the beer is still foaming up over the edge of the cup and down his hairy hand, he chugs the contents in a series of quick gulps, before filling the cup again and scowling silently at it.

One of the other guys leans over to Big Jim and says, "What was *that* all about?", to which Jim just shakes his head slowly and says "Don't even *ask* about this one."

As the men chat, Kai looks around and notices that he is one of the few slender people at the barbeque today. Although they are generally in their thirties and forties, the majority of men and women there are at different stages of being overweight, some just starting to fill out in the upper arms and neck, with others well on their way to severe obesity – as though they might lift up into the air and float away like a balloon at any moment.

The trim European is reminded of a set of colorful, hand-painted nesting dolls he had seen once in an antique shop. It was a set of hollow wooden figures, pear-shaped and bulging out at the bottom. They were all the same shape, but each one was progressively larger than the next, so that one could fit into the other, until they all disappeared in sequence into the belly of the largest of them all.

Wondering who at this party would serve the role of that last, largest doll into which all the rest would disappear, Kai's eyes fall suddenly upon a woman across the yard who is chattering at a rapid pace with Wendy and a few others: the woman's knees look like tight, little sugar dots about to be engulfed by the overflowing masses of her thighs and calves.

Kai himself wears a medium.

At a lull that follows the men's conversation about the "Big Game on Sunday" that will be on TV, Big Jim proclaims, "Well, it's time to start grillin'!", and they all start to shift over to the patio where the barbeque is.

Distracted by this movement from across the lawn, Jim's Rottweiler charges over to them and starts jumping on and pawing at one guest after another. As the hound lunges onto Alex and starts licking him with his slobbering tongue from chin to temple, painting him with saliva, Alex lifts his beer up above himself to safety. As the two of them perform what looks like a discordant fox trot, the beer sloshes out of the cup and crashes like a sloppy wave against Alex's shoulders and torso, drenching him.

"Damn it!!", Alex shouts, as his brother bellows to the dog "Rock! DOWN!! *DOWN*, Rock!! SIT! I said *SIT*!", and little by little, the corpulent dog starts to ease himself into a temporary crouch, his tongue still hanging from his jaws and flailing about, in rhythm to the heaving of the dog's massive chest.

With his finger raised and his arm lifted at the shoulder, Jim stares at the dog with a look of domineering defiance, as if this is the last warning. After a pause, and with the dog in a barely contained squat, Jim suddenly smiles and melts into a "GOOD dog, Rock. THAT'S a good dog", rubbing the animal's head briskly between the ears.

Proud to have shown the other men that he is the boss of this ominous pile of tooth and muscle in front of them, Jim turns and continues leading the others to the grill. Once his back is turned, the dog springs up again from his holding pattern and bites into the shorts leg of the man in the back of the group, playfully tugging and shaking his own, thick head back and forth frantically.

At the grill, which has already been prepared for the occasion and is now radiating a pleasant warmth, Big Jim calls out to his wife to gather the crowd about him.

"Hon?", he shouts across the yard, waving the barbeque tongs to her, "Let's get it on!"

Wendy starts chattering more excitedly with the people around her, corralling everyone into an exodus of guests that waddle leisurely in their oversized shorts, armless shirts and sandals to the barbeque, the largest woman following with great effort at the rear.

Once everyone has more or less gathered about him in a mass, Jim distributes a benevolent smile and raises the barbeque tongs to the heavens.

"Lord", he shouts upwards to the sky, "Bless this barbeque, and grant us sunshine and good weather, so that our friends and family may eat and drink, in celebration of the name of Christ!"

As Jim's arms are raised, his brother-in-law positions his phone and takes a picture of the great moment, with himself in the foreground and the host at the barbeque in the background (a selfie for Jesus).

Big Jim holds his arms aloft for a moment longer, and realizing that nothing further is coming (either from himself or from the attentive heavens above), he lowers his head and releases a quiet and humble "Amen", as if he is ashamed.

And the members of the crowd among him lower their heads and mumble "Amen" in a quiet, disorderly unison, as though something beautiful and of great significance has just occurred.

Then, Jim reaches with the tips of the barbeque tongs to the pile of meat beside him, lifts up a steak dripping with red-orange sauce (which happens to also include his secret chili ingredient), and shouts to the assembled congregation, "Let's *EAT*!!", to which there is a resounding roar and applause.

Smiling with tremendous satisfaction at his having been sufficiently pious without losing his ability to be loose and carefree, Jim slaps the meat onto the grill, and a flame shoots up from around it, high on all sides, as the flesh of the sacrificial animal begins to sizzle and burn.

As the celebrants bubble again into their respective chatter and shuffle back to their earlier places in the yard, the expat from Europe stands silently and motionlessly amongst them.

What he has just witnessed is entirely foreign to him. He and his people in the North of Germany are protestant, and aside from the requisite events, like Christmas and confirmation, as well as keeping the church clean and free of any colorful distractions, there hasn't been much more to it.

This role of religion in day-to-day life is something that Kai had not yet seen in the "Company Buddy" that had been assigned to him at his workplace.

"*SO*, Kai", Big Jim bursts out heartily from the grill, waking the expat from a reflective stupor and, at this point, frightening him a little.

Kai turns to his host, who is poised over the grill imposingly, as though he himself is the only one amongst them who possesses the manliness and stamina necessary to face the heat and flip the burgers, steaks and frankfurters.

"That's a heck of a pickle we're in with the X-15 project at the office, ain't it?", Jim says, as he shifts the meat around in place on the grill.

"Yes, dat is kvite a pickle", Kai agrees, as his eyes suddenly fall on a giant jar of pickles that also happens to be on a stand next to the grill.

"Increased performance at a competitive price!", Jim says, standing erect and wriggling his upper torso back and forth, as he mockingly repeats the phrase from the "Team Workshop" in which they were updated as to current market conditions.

Rubbing his chin and looking off reflectively, the European colleague says quietly and out loud, as if to himself, "I sink it vould be a good idea to research der matter furser. Perhaps to have another meeting vit der engineers from der other department. Den, a meeting vit the budgeting office. Den, of course, dare vill need to be anosser meeting of der engineers to discuss der findings, and den to perhaps consider…"

"Oh, we don't have to go overboard about it", his Company Buddy interrupts, calmly working at the meat. "We'll just get a rough idea and put whatever we have out on the market next week like we planned, before the competition gets a jump on us… If we don't, we'll *never* come out on top."

Jim sees his "Company Buddy" looking at him with an expression of apprehension.

"We can always tweak everything a little later, as we go along… No sweat!", Big Jim says, casually flipping a burger high above the grill.

Observing his coworker, Kai notices a pool of perspiration soaking into the tank top just below Big Jim's armpits.

In all of his engineering studies at his university in Germany, Kai never once was confronted with the scientific method of "tweaking". He recently heard about "twerking" on the television the other night, and he wonders if that is in any way the same thing.

Then, against his will, Kai has an image in his head of Big Jim sweating in his tank top as he crouches and throbs his bulky hips up and down like the girl in the video did on the television, and the European wonders how exactly that will help them resolve their problem with the X-15 project.

"Pow!", goes a sudden explosion.

Kai's eyes fix upon the gas tank below the grill, then "Pow! Pow Pow!"

"Bart, cut it out with those things!", Big Jim shouts at his son, who has a handful of little tufts of twirled paper in his hands that he has been smashing against the patio floor. The papers are filled with explosive powder, and they make a loud bang as they make contact.

"They just pop, dad. They don't do anything!", the fifteen-year-old boy says.

"I don't give a rat's dang", the father scolds. "I said quit throwing them things all over the place."

"Awright", the boy drones, as he pouts and slumps off.

Then Big Jim returns to his conversation with his coworker, and a few moments later, there is a slightly distant "Pop! Pop Pop!" from another part of the yard.

Lifting up a plate of burgers and franks, Jim says to Kai and the other guys, "I'm gonna go bring these to the girls", referring to his wife Wendy and the women with whom she is sitting, all of whom are well into their forties and have children.

"Oh, we're still doing it", Wendy says at the table before Jim arrives, as she exchanges a sly smile with her sister-in-law. "Don't gemme wrong. It just take's Jim a little longer to get in the mood, that's all."

"I know what ya' mean", her sister-in-law responds, waving a hand at Wendy. "Tom's been that way for a while. I think it's stress from work."

"Have ya' tried Viagra?", Wendy asks sweetly.

"We're thinkin' about it. Tom's not too happy about the idea, but I'm gonna see what I can do."

Jim approaches from across the yard with the heaping, steaming plate.

As he appears at the table, he holds up a foot-long frankfurter with the tongs and says, "Can I interest you ladies in a hot piece of meat?". He says it in an overly deep voice, like an Elvis impersonator, as he raises his eyebrows flirtatiously.

The women all giggle hysterically, and Wendy slaps his thick upper arm and says, "Oh, Jim!" as she laughs.

The women all laugh to each other, and Jim assumes it is at his subtly crafted innuendo.

"I'm ready for *my* piece of meat", Wendy then says to him, and she turns to the women and they all laugh again, loud and shrill.

"You got it, baby", Big Jim says to her, laying the plump, lengthy frankfurter on the plate in front of her and then placing the platter in the center of the table. Then, he smiles to the group of women like a grand Casanova before strutting back to the barbeque with manly pride.

Back at the grill, Jim's brother Alex looks over the rim of his red plastic cup and then says to Jim, "What the hell was *that* all about!".

"Oh, just horsin' 'round a little", he says, smiling with satisfaction at his recent performance as he turns back to the grill.

Alex watches the women at their table across the yard. He can see that one of them leans in to the others and says something while she looks over in the direction of the barbeque, and then they all break out in their hysterical laughter again.

Alex scowls at them and takes another swig from his giant cup. He has already moved on to whiskey, straight, after taking a slight detour through boiler-makers.

He is distracted by a conversation that has started up amongst the guys, who are surrounding Jim and watching as he mans the barbeque.

"It's terrible what's happening to this country", one of the men says.

"Vat do you mean?", the European expat asks.

"Nobody cares about anything anymore", one of the other men chimes in. "Everybody wants to get something for nothing. Like they're entitled."

Then they all look at the cooking meat, eager for the steaks to be done.

"All those people pourin' in over the border. It's like we're being invaded!"

"And they all expect to just be handed everything once they get here."

"Like that *Obama*care!", one of them says, and the men all scowl at each other.

"It's disgusting!", Alex erupts.

Standing quietly amongst them, the European expat remembers a television report he saw about an American family; they developed a 250,000-dollar debt because one of their children had a blood infection. Then, Kai recalls a time when he had a kidney stone that had to be handled by his urologist. The stone was broken up with a big machine that emitted some kind of waves, and the entire procedure cost him a 20 euro copayment.

While the men complain about what has become of their society, Jim's son Bart has been hanging around on the fringes of the group, playing with a red, translucent fidget spinner in the sunlight.

"There's a kid in school, and his parents are vegetarians", the boy informs the men, as if informing the authorities about an injustice that might perhaps need to be punished.

"Holy crap!", Alex blurts out, and the other guys laugh about the ridiculous parents. Bart watches his father Big Jim press the meat tighter to the grill, searing the flesh and making the juice squirt out into the flames.

"OK!", Jim announces to the guys assembled around him, "who's in the mood for a coupla' steaks?"

The men all stand instantly upright, ready for action. Big Jim peels off one steak after another from the line of meat that has been grilling on the metal strips of the barbeque, and he lays each one gently with the tongs onto the nearest plate that is held out to him.

After their plate has been filled, each grateful recipient heads over to the table on the other side of the barbeque, reaches a big serving spoon into the potato salad and slaps a dollop next to the steak. Then, there are the sticky, red-drown baked beans, which are dropped down in the remaining free area. This is followed by an ear of corn, which most of the guys generally place lengthwise across the steak, to solve the little matter of remaining space. A couple of them then go right for the pudding (there is chocolate and a separate bowl of some very yellow vanilla – another of Wendy's instant concoctions). Some of the guys lift the ketchup over the steak and shake the bottle in stabbing motions until the glutinous, red mixture comes out, and some opt for the Worcestershire sauce.

They all walk back to the area around the grill, trying to balance their respective pile so that the various sauces, juices and fluids (which have all by now started to run together) don't drip down the fluted sides of the paper plates – then, it would be wasted.

Now settled into place around the grill, each man stands as he holds his plate in one hand while he shovels a little plastic forkful of baked beans, then one of potato salad, and maybe another of pudding (as an interim desert, before moving back to the rest) into his open, chewing mouth. Then they look around and find a TV tray here, the edge of a cement wall there to rest their plates on as they start to cut the steak with the little, serrated plastic knives.

"These things are too small", Alex says, and then he adds, "oh, ta' hell with it!", and he grabs his steak in his hands and lifts it up to his mouth for a big "Chomp!". He smiles with big, wide eyes and a silly grin at the other guys, while thin lines of brown and yellow sauce drip down along the sides of his chin.

The guys all smile back in grateful appreciation at this act of freedom and libertinism. One of them then throws his little plastic knife over his shoulder, picks up his steak with his hand and chops into it likewise, and the other guys follow gleefully along. Jim has joined in, as has his son Bart, and the father and son look at each other over their fists full of steak and exchange a glance of deep bonding, as if to say, "This is one of those great moments that we'll remember forever, ain't it!".

Meanwhile, Kai has returned with his plate of one frankfurter and a little mustard, a small spoonful of potato salad and another of baked beans. He seats himself at a nearby garden chair, out of earshot of the group, with his legs crossed and his plate in his lap, where he slices a piece of the frankfurter with his plastic knife and fork, dips it lightly into the dab of mustard, and looks around the garden vacantly as he releases a sigh and chews.

After the steak and the corn on the cob, the tongs of the little plastic forks have come to be greatly appreciated by the American men for their dual use as toothpicks, and the guys stand amongst each other with the sides of their upper lips raised, as they twist and excavate to get the strands and chunks out. These are either re-chewed and gratefully swallowed, or spit out abruptly to the side.

Meanwhile, Rock the Rottweiler has come bucking along, and Big Jim seizes the occasion by saying, "Hey guys, ya' gotta check this out!".

Then, Jim rips a hunk from a cooked hamburger, holds it in the tips of his thumb and index finger in front of the hound's face and raises a firm finger with the other hand, pulling the morsel back as the dog reaches for it.

"Rock, sit. I said SIT! *SIT*, boy!", and the dog wriggles himself into a sitting position as he lets out a libidinous yelp.

Then, Jim reaches and places the piece of cooked hamburger tenderly on the top of the Rottweiler's dark snout, an inch away from the dog's wet, black nose. The dog can smell it – the cooked meat, the savory flesh of the other animal, as the aroma seeps into his twitching, black nostrils.

"Noooo", Jim drawls in a tone of warning, "No, Rock, nooooo, waaaaait, nooooo…"

The men are enraptured at the sight. There are a few chortles and giggles as they enjoy the moment of animalistic tension, and Jim's brother-in-law has started to film the event on his phone.

The dog has started to whimper. He is clearly being pushed ever closer to the threshold of his self control, to that place in his psyche where attack and submit, lunge and obey live in a precarious balance to each other.

"Noooo", Jim says, "nooooo… OKAY, Rock! NOW!!", and the dog's sharp jaws toss the cooked hamburger up into the air and then snap at it, capturing it and chewing it gratefully and desperately, as the men all laugh and applaud.

"Good boy, Rock. *GOOD* boy!", Jim says, rubbing the beast's head and pressing it downwards somewhat as the meat is chewed, not at all concerned about the very fine line upon which he himself had been teetering, crouched as he was there in front of the muscular Rottweiler as it was pushed to the edge.

"He's a good dog", Jim says, turning to his crew. "A big, powerful, black animal. That's why we named him the Rock!"

The other guys all laugh as they exchange a glance of brotherhood at the playful reference to race and color.

"Too bad *all* black creatures aren't as good as Rock is", one of the guys says to the group.

"Yea, Rock knows how to handle himself."

"They got everything goin' for 'em, in the greatest country in the world, and they *still* can't get it together", one of the men adds.

"Yea, just say you're half black, and you can walk right into any college and get a job in any company you want, no matter how many other guys are waitin' in line", another responds.

"It's so unfair!", Alex says moodily, shaking his head and taking another gulp of whisky.

Now, these particular men are not the kind to burn cigar holes into white pillow cases and use them as hoods on midnight rides through the village, enforcing mob justice. They even view themselves as being fair and open-minded. They are, however, themselves colored in regard to their opinions – and that color is not the color of the democracy of which they claim to be so proud.

What these men born with white skin have neglected to consider is the fact that American society has been honed and organized for centuries to keep people born with brown skin from being permitted the conditions to live the life of educated, independent human beings, let alone having an equal role in their own homeland – with the overall result not being particularly surprising.

These men have overlooked the fact that sometimes the white schools were endowed with microscopes while the schools for black kids just got more tools to prepare them for the manual labor professions[2], and the fact that at one period in their glorious democracy, people with brown skin were not allowed to register to vote without answering the question "How many bubbles are there in a bar of soap?".

In fact, the tragedy is even worse – while these particular men view themselves as being superior to their darker-skinned countrymen, they themselves don't even know about these events from their own country's history.

They know about Trayvon Martin, though...

Just as Big Jim is saying something about the prison population, a man comes through the gate and walks toward the small group at the barbeque.

With his eyes now fixed upon the entering figure, Jim holds onto the collar of his dog and says "S-S-S-SIT!", in a firm, solid tone.

---

[2] Angelou, Maya <u>I Know Why the Caged Bird Sings</u>

Every other pair of eyes near the grill, as well as every pair of eyes elsewhere in the backyard, become focused upon the man as his presence is noticed in turn.

There is a brief pause in the conversations, and then they resume, in a different tone, before returning to the collection of chatter and loud laughter as before. Meanwhile, from the groups of mothers and aunts, fathers, brothers and sisters, glances are cast at the young man with brown skin, who is wearing a button-down shirt and smiling as he enters their party.

"Jordan!", the European expat calls out to him, waving his hand as he stands and smiles.

Jordan walks over to Kai and they exchange a friendly handshake as they begin to talk together.

The other men near the barbeque exchange with each other a quiet look of suspicion.

Being the host, Big Jim is the one to walk over to Kai and the new entrant, after he sends Rock away with a sharp whistle and a smack on the haunches.

"Hello there", Jim says in a friendly tone with a big smile on his face and an extended hand. "I'm Jim."

Kai takes it upon himself to handle the rest of the introductions.

"Jim, I vould like to introduce you to Jordan", he says, happy to be doing the honors. "He lives in my apartment building. Jordan, dat is Jim, und dat here is his house."

"Hello, Jim", Jordan says, taking the offered hand and shaking it. "It's nice to meet you".

"Same here", Jim says. Then, he turns abruptly to the other guys behind him and says, "Guys, this here is Jordan, a friend of Kai's", even though they were right there and could hear everything that had been said.

As if suddenly realizing that their scowling faces can be seen from the outside, they unscrew their expressions and replace them with cordial smiles, as they raise their palms and say hello.

Kai and Jordan chat together with Jim – about the apartment building, about Kai being from Germany, and such obvious things.

"Well," Jim finally says, being the good host, and realizing there is no way to postpone the matter, "Are you in the mood for a hamburger, Jordan?"

Jordan smiles appreciatively at Jim and says, "I'm *starving*!", and then they both walk over to the grill.

As Jim turns back to Kai with a somewhat questioning look, the expat says innocently, "You told me I should bring somebody," wondering if he has somehow misunderstood the finer points of the invitation.

As Jordan thanks Jim for the hamburger, he walks over to the group of men.

No longer able to talk behind the curtain, so to speak, the men chat openly with the newcomer.

"Great day for a barbeque, ain't it?", Jim's brother-in-law says.

"It sure is", Jordan agrees, smiling up at the sky and then taking a bite of the hamburger.

"We only have meat. We don't have any fried chicken or anything like that", the brother-in-law adds, in an attempt to be friendly.

The new guest pauses mid bite, looks at the man who just spoke to him, and then continues with his burger.

"That's O.K.", Jordan says. "Burgers are fine."

"They said it was supposta rain today", somebody else adds. "Looks like we lucked out."

"Yea", Jordan agrees. "But it sure is hot".

The man standing next to Alex has a puzzled look on his face, and then he asks Jordan, "Do you guys get hot in the sun?".

Jordan pauses again, then he finishes his last bite, wipes his fingertips lightly against each other, and looks at the man.

"Who?", Jordan asks.

"I don't know… black people. Do you guys get hot in the sun, too?"

The question is asked not with aggression, but more with a child's curiosity about the unknown.

After a reflective moment, Jordan politely informs the man, "Yes, we get hot."

"Oh", the other man says, as though finding this piece of information to be particularly interesting. Then, he sees Alex scowling at him, and he says, "I was just asking!".

Jordan looks at the men for a moment, and then he turns to Kai and strikes up a pleasant conversation about their apartment group, which then morphs into a discussion about music.

As the dialogue turns to jazz recordings that they both enjoy, Kai looks in the direction of the group and notices that the other guys still look a little apprehensive for some reason.

96

Then, as Jordan goes to the table for some potato salad and baked beans, Kai leans over to Jim at the grill and whispers in his ear.

"It is OK", the European says. "He is not a contractor", remembering what he had been told on his first day of work by the Human Resources representative.

The Fundraiser

"Don't eat all of it!", Wendy calls out to her son Bart, who is wiping a fingerful of the instant brownie mixture from the bowl and sticking it into his mouth. "That's for the church fundraiser!", she says.

As the boy twists around the end of the breakfast bar headed for the backyard, he darts like a runningback around his father, who appears suddenly from the entrance of the master bedroom.

Waddling into the great room and standing in front of the blaring television, Big Jim pulls the flaps of his pants together, buttons them and laces his belt into the clasp.

"Whacha got there, hon?", he says, after the shaving cream commercial loses his interest.

"Home-made brownies for this afternoon!"

"Ooh!", Jim says. He turns and reaches over the breakfast bar, sticks his finger into the pale-brown mixture and throws the dollop into his gaping mouth.

Wendy looks at his face with eager anticipation.

"Yum!", her husband says, his eyebrows dancing upwards as he smiles at her.

Wendy stirs briskly with a satisfied smile. Then she looks at the mixture, turns to the directions on the box and reads, scowling from the box to the mixture and then back to the box, as if something, somewhere, must have gone wrong.

Then she rips her head upwards suddenly at the shocking noise as the TV is switched from the morning chat program to the celebrity entertainment show.

The teenage girl drops the remote control and lets it bounce carelessly on the sofa cushion. She is wearing painfully tight short-shorts, with deep gashes ripped into the remaining fabric of the legs and with the white cloth of the inner pockets sticking through.

After watching the changing colors and flashing lights of the program for a few moments, she swirls her body around on the spot. Then, she struts across the room as if training for her great moment on a catwalk or red carpet someday soon, whenever that moment finally comes. At the sliding door to the yard, she stops abruptly, shifts her slender weight from one hip to the other, and observes the result in the reflection.

"That's what yer gonna wear to the church fundraiser?", Wendy asks her.

The 16-year-old whips her face around without moving her shoulders. She stares firmly and then smiles with a look of self-satisfaction at her mother, before rolling her own eyes upwards with a boredom and world-weariness that can only be experienced either by an American middle-class girl between the ages of 15 and 17, or someone who has lost everything in a long, drawn-out war.

"Oh, Mom. You're *so-o-o* out of fashion", the girl drawls.

The doorbell rings, and the girl pivots towards the entrance door expectantly, wondering who it is who is going to see her.

Jim answers the door with a hearty "Well, hello, buddy! Common in!", and Kai enters holding a plastic briefcase in one hand.

"Good morning, Jim. Hello Vendy", Kai says.

"Hey, Kai!", Wendy waves exuberantly back and forth from the kitchen area a few feet away.

The facial features of the teenage girl relax into a posture of boredom and disappointment, and she remains posed at the sliding door, watching the television screen to her side.

"Sank you, Jim, for der power drill", Kai says, handing his acquaintance the plastic briefcase with the blue handle.

"Oh, no problem, dude," Jim says, accepting the briefcase. "Any time."

Kai looks at the girl across from him, and Wendy says, "Oh, Kai, this is our daughter, Jasmine!".

"Hello, Jasmine. It is nice to meet you", the European says.

The girl turns again to the door and flashes her best on-camera smile and says "Hello". She might as well use the opportunity to practice, she figures, since it's just one of her Dad's nerdy old-man friends from work.

"Jassmeen", Kai repeats. "Dat is a nice name. Der vas a jassmeen plant by my window ven I vas on vacation in Majorca. The aroma vas so sveet and pleasant," he says, smiling to Wendy in appreciation of her choice of name for her child.

Wendy puts the bowl down on the countertop and stares at Kai with a blank expression.

"Yea...", she says vacantly. "We named her after the Disney character."

The European expat returns her expression, and is interrupted by Jim's invitation for Kai to join them at the fundraiser.

"Oh, sank you, but no", Kai smiles humbly. "Jordan vill help me today to move some furniture in my apartment", he says.

At the mention of the brown-skinned neighbor that Kai brought to the barbeque last weekend, Jim clears his throat with a gravely sound.

Then, he smiles at Kai and says, "Cool!", puts his hand on Kai's back and turns with him towards the entrance.

"Goodbye, Vendy. Goodbye, Jassmeen", Kai says over his shoulder, as Jim is guiding him through the front door.

"So long, Kai!", Wendy says. Jasmine raises a few fingers and lowers them, as if whisking away a mosquito, as she continues to watch the celebrities on the big screen in front of her.

After Kai leaves, the phone rings. Wendy wipes her hands on the kitchen towel and answers.

It's Wendy's sister.

"Hey, sis", she says. "Hold on a second." Then to Jasmine, "Don't let your brother eat all the brownie mix!", without waiting for any response and then heading herself into the master bedroom as she chats on the phone.

"I'll be in the garage", Jim says to the television screen before going out the front door.

As the front door slams shut, the patio door to the backyard slides open and Bart rushes in, headed for the kitchen area.

"Mom said don't eat all the brownie mix", Jasmine says mundanely to the screen.

Her brother repeats what she says with a snotty tone to his voice as he takes another fingerful of the brownie mixture.

"You goin', too?", he asks her.

"Yea", she says. "Another boring Saturday."

"Yea", the boy says.

Then, Jasmine smiles deviously.

"HEY", she shouts, and then whispering, "I know how we can liven it up a little!".

Then she rushes into her bedroom, and after another fingerful of the mixture, her brother sees her scamper back out like a giddy schoolgirl and over to the kitchen.

She has a little clear-plastic bag in her hands. She opens it, plucks something out and scatters it over the brownie mix.

"What are you doin'?", Bart asks her with an eager smile.

"Nothin'", Jasmine says as she stirs.

"What is that?"

"It's pot, stupid!", his sister says, giggling to her brother like she used to when they played together in the backyard as kids.

Bart's eyes stretch wide open.

"No way!", he says to his sister, with a gaping smile.

"We gotta do *somethin'* to get the party started", she says.

Then, Bart's expression turns to one of worry.

"But pot's illegal... ain't it?"

"It's legal, doofus. Don't you watch T.V.?"

102

What the girl has not gathered from her hodgepodge consumption of media is that marijuana is only legal for medical purposes in the state she and her family live in… and she is completely unaware that it is still illegal in other parts of the country.

"Oh… then I'll just tell Mom and Dad", her brother says, sauntering casually away from the breakfast bar in no particular direction.

"DON'T!", his sister shouts.

"Why not? If it's legal?"

His sister looks at him, and then she rolls her eyes and looks away.

"I don't think Jim and Wendy are gonna' like the whole congregation getting' stoned", she says.

Bart starts laughing at the idea.

"Yea!… heh heh… heh", he says, chortling repeatedly.

"Don't tell!", she shouts at him, and she holds her right pinky up in the air. After a pause, he raises *his* right pinky, and they wrap their two fingers together in the form of bond that they used to use when they shared secrets years ago.

The deal is done.

Jasmine finishes whipping up the heady concoction, and they both squeal and rush around the breakfast bar and leap over the back of the couch, landing with a thump just as their mother comes back into the great room and says "OK, see ya' there!" into the phone before hanging up.

The brother and sister look secretively at each other and break out is a rash of suppressed giggles, their foreheads close to each other on the sofa.

Their mother eyes them suspiciously.

"What's with you two?", she says, pouring the spiked brownie mixture into the glass form, and not being surprised that it is, as usual, somehow rather clumpy.

"Oh, just su-um funny on T.V.", the sister says, certain from experience that her excuse will not be challenged or pursued.

And they stare fixedly at the screen until their mother gets distracted and moves on.

———————————————

As the family of four climb out of the SUV in the church parking lot, they see the separate area that is intended for the car wash this afternoon – there are several buckets full of soapy water, a bunch of giant sponges next to them, and a hose that runs to the back of the church building.

On the big sign, right under the printed blue words "Church of Our Holy Virgin", there are the exchangeable black letters that read, "Car Wash Today!!", and then, underneath, the offer "Cleanliness and Godliness – Get Your Two-for-One!".

The pastor walks towards them and greets them, his gold watch shining in the sun as he waves.

Wendy holds up her tray to him, as if making an offering at an alter.

"Homemade brownies, Father!", she calls to him.

"Oh", the priests says, taking them and looking benevolently at them, as if they are a newly born babe. "They look heavenly."

Bart casts a worried look at his sister, who then gives him a devious little smile.

The brownies are put together on a long table with the other baked goods, snacks, cola bottles and coffee, and the dozen or so members of the congregation start to break into groups and chat as they take a bite here and there.

As the first car rolls up to the car wash area, everyone turns – first suspiciously, as if their social event is being intruded upon, and then almost immediately (remembering why they are there) with jubilation at their first customer, who has admitted to himself that he and his car are soiled enough to need to come to them and be cleansed.

Bart and the other teenage boys break apart like a football squad, waddling with the buckets of water closer to the car and plying their budding muscles to their task at hand.

"Our first soul!", the preacher says, finishing off his brownie and heading over to greet the new client.

After a few steps, he turns back and calls out to Wendy, "Great brownies!", flashing a thumbs-up, which she gleefully returns with both thumbs.

After a robust polishing with dry cloths, the driver slips his bill into the slot in the milky-white bucket under the sign "Pay here!", and he thanks everyone and drives off.

Then the boys stand around with the sponges in their hands, ready for further deployment, and after watching the cars come and go at the traffic light and pass them by, their eager posture starts to slump into one of disuse. A few empty buckets are overturned and sat upon, and the original glow of their early business success starts to fade.

One of the boys gets tired of waiting and goes over to the snack table, where the priest and the others are chatting and feeding.

"It's a little slow, Father", the boy says, with a complaining tone. "Nobody else is comin'".

"Ye-e-e-e-s", the pastor says, as if he has been presented with a spiritual conundrum and is reflecting upon the most pious solution.

"Perhaps we should have someone on the street, holding a sign... to kind of *tempt* them a little", the priest adds.

"Cool idea, Father!", the boy shouts, his faith in the carwash event now re-inspired.

"There's some paper and some magic markers in the rectory", the reverend says. "Why don't you and the other boys go and make up something really, really cooooool", he says, lowering his eyelids and then taking a bite of his next brownie.

The boy looks studiously at his holy leader for a moment, and then says, "OK, we're on it!", and he bounces off to the group of boys to bring reinforcements along to the rectory.

Wendy's sister is there, and she tells the pastor about the registration list for Sunday school classes.

"And it the Johnsons' kids both sign on, we'll have a full group this month", she says, before taking another bite of her brownie.

The pastor chews silently, nodding his head, and then raises his eyebrows and lets out a slow, lugubrious, "Wi-i-i-i-ld".

Wendy and her sister look at each other, and then Wendy says, "Yea, that *is* wild!", and the woman laugh together, with the pastor smiling and chewing.

"Re-e-e-a-l w-i-i-i-i-ld", he says, smiling now, and they all laugh together uncontrollably.

"And then we'll need to get more folding chairs!", Wendy's sister shouts, laughing at her own suggestion.

The preacher smiles as he repeats for her his "Wi-i-i-i-ld", at which they all bust out into a fit of hysteria, as if they had just been waiting for it. Then, the laughter gathers a momentum of its own and they just start laughing at each other for having laughed, and there are gasps for breath during the laughter, and people buckling over with laughter, and a hand or two slapping the table top during the laughter, and then they each start trying to come up with other things to say about the Sunday school to get a new reaction out of the pastor.

"And we'll need *pencils*!", Wendy shouts, holding her remaining half of a brownie up in the air victoriously, at which the pastor says, "Co-o-o-ol", and the laughter kicks back in again.

It's silly laughter now, and the woman next to Wendy stops giggling suddenly, opens her eyes wide, juts a pointed index finger into the air and burst out with, "And we'll have to *sharpen* 'em!", at which everybody in the group doubles over with laughter.

"Wh...wh...whaddaya think about *that*, Father?", Wendy says, gasping for breath amidst her howls and roars.

"Me?", the reverend says, smiling mischievously at his little congregation at the snack table. "Well, I'll just tell you a little su-um 'bout that", and the women bubble as they emit barely suppressed giggles.

"I think…", the pastor says, and then leaves a long, dramatic pause as he looks at his listeners, who are clearly eager to erupt at any moment, "…that *sharpened PENcils"*, he teasingly adds (and Wendy's sister starts shaking with the laughter that she is trying to not let out) "…are the *most…imPORtant…*".

Now the preacher dons a look of gravity and severity, and he looks from the eyes of one of the giggling, jiggling women to the next, and then he repeats, "… the *most…imPORtant…*", and then, he shouts as he throws his hand up into the air "*POINT!!"*.

And the small group of women and the preacher start to howl and stomp around on the ground in front of the nearly empty brownie tray: "BWAAAA!!", "OH, OH, OH", and then one of the women inhales as she says the words "Oh my God!" and the party of intoxicated believers roars louder and more raucously than before.

Their husbands at the other end of the table look over and smile to each other.

"What's goin' on over there?", one of them says.

"I donno", says Big Jim, "but it looks a lot more fun than the sermon was last Sunday", at which the guys chuckle quietly.

Meanwhile, the small deployment of teenage boys has returned with the sign, and one of them looks around and says, "OK, who wants to go out on the side of the street and hold it up?".

"*I'M* not doin' it", Bart says, and then offers as his excuse, "I helped make the sign".

"*I* don't want everybody starin' at me all afternoon", one of the other boys says.

At that moment, Jasmine's eyes ricochet towards the boys by the other side of the driveway, and her head and body spin and follow.

"*I'LL* do it!", she shouts, her eyes burning with an inner fire. She says it as if the votes have now been cast and her role as the sign-holder is unshakable.

She eyeballs the 17-year-old boy who is holding the sign, as if to burn a whole through him.

Then, she struts her most practiced of struts to him and r-r-r-ips the sign out of his hand, before pivoting on cue (the cue that is in her own head, of course) and striding to the entrance of the church driveway, stomping one sneakered foot in the middle of her own path and then the next, like a cat, as if she is simply fabulous and the phone is going to start blistering with calls from one modeling agency after another at any moment.

When she gets out to the side of the street, she stands and looks with a self-satisfied glare at the passing traffic – her public – and she throws her arms up into the air to broadcast her message.

"Car Wash! 5 Bucks", the sign says.

Jasmine stands like that for a few minutes, eyeballing each passing driver with a look that says, "*You* know you want your car washed, and I know it, too… let's stop kidding ourselves".

Then, after a while, she turns defiantly in the sandy roadside to face the oncoming lane of traffic as she *juts* the sign high again into the air, as if she is screaming it.

A disconsolate, forsaken look soon appears on her face, and her arms lower slowly with the sign… THEN she stands sharply and pivots in place in the sand, strides back to the waiting boys and says, "Hold this", flicking the sign disinterestedly to one of them. "I have an idea."

And she walks off to the church building and disappears inside.

After a forlorn period of time in the hot summer sun, one of the boys looks up again towards the church. His mouth gapes, and he prods his buddy next to him with his elbow.

"Whoa!", the second boy says, and they all watch Jasmine as she struts back defiantly from the church building in her hot-pink bikini, which is more pink than it is bikini.

She walks straight towards them with her step - step - step rhythm, eyeballing them. As she arrives, she tears the sign out of the boy's hand (they're in the same math class at school) and struts to the roadside.

She passes the adults at the snack table at a distance, and they watch her as she goes. The preacher lets out an "Oh, sweet Lord" and makes the sign of the cross in her direction.

The sixteen-year-old takes her position back on the roadside, and moments after she has jutted her sign up into the air again and struck a bold pose, a car swerves and barely misses her before screeching to a halt.

She gives the driver a "what's wrong with you?!" sneer, but when she sees the young man just staring back at her, as if captivated and without the powers of speech or independent thought, she smiles at him, knowing that she has now hit upon her own secret formula.

She juts the sign high up into the air again, and she wiggles her hips a little here and shakes her upper torso a little there. As one car passes by, she just shifts her weight from one hip to the other, and the car rolls into the church parking lot, as if drawn by magnetic force. In another car approaching the stoplight, a male driver seems to by trying not to look, so she rolls her shoulders and rotates her torso… and he's in.

It's like fishing – with a big, wide net.

Cars are honk-honk-ho-o-onking as they pass through the green light at full speed, and there are shouts out of car windows, some of which are audible, some of which are not, and many of which have never been shouted to the Church of Our Holy Virgin before.

As one car turns into the driveway after another, the boys are hustling and bustling to service their clientele. In spite of their speed and energy, there is a long line building, which is now curving out the parking lot and into the entrance by the road.

Cash is being shoved in the slot of the plastic collection bucket, the boys are given tips, and everybody – *EVERY*-body – has their eyes – on – Jasmine… as she stands in her bikini on the roadside and holds the "Car Wash! 5 Bucks" sign high into the air, as only she can.

The traffic light turns red, and an elderly couple in a car approaches it slowly. The grandfatherly figure at the wheel is staring past his wife through the closed window at Jasmine and her hot-pink mini-bikini, and there is a sudden "FLUMP!" as his car rolls into the one that is stopped in front of him at the traffic light. From the passenger side, the grandmotherly figure starts slapping him on the shoulder and side of the head with her magazine, and she is clearly shouting at him inside the closed car.

Jasmine is quite pleased with herself – but after a few moments, it is not enough... and she wants more.

From her place by the roadside, she calls out over her shoulder, to no one in particular, "Get the suds!"

"What?", the boy nearest to her shouts.

"I said get the suds. Bring 'em over here!"

The boy looks at her for a moment, and then he summons the assistance of his coworker. In a matter of minutes, the two boys waddle over, each with two buckets of soapy water in their hands, and they drop them down at her feet, with a splash.

Then she smiles to them deviously and says "Suds me!", looking straight into the eyes of the boys, to a place in them that they themselves will not discover yet for another year or so.

The two boys throw their hands with the thick sponges into the buckets, and as they pull them out, the sudsy water follows their movements in arching streams as they apply the big car sponges to the teenage girl, squeezing the water over her shoulders as it drips down he arms, her clavicles, and soaks into the cloth of her hot-pink string bikini.

One boy reaches his hands over her head to squeeze out a giant spongeful of soapy water, and Jasmine suddenly steps aside and turns to him as she shouts "*Not in my hair!!*".

Yes, many drivers today – young, old and everything in between – are glaring at the teenager's bare skin, dripping with soapy foam in the hot summer sun near the sign for the Church of Our Holy Virgin.

And the church is raking in the cash.

Ready to kick things up a notch, Jasmine turns and smiles as she whispers something to the boy from her math class, and he runs like a rocket into the rectory.

Moments later, he returns, and he hands her the new sign she has requested: "Selfies - $10!!".

She holds both signs up, and the offer is a huge success. Teenagers and men of various ages and backgrounds stop, put their arm around her, with her covered in suds, and pose for a selfie, using their own phones.

As her star continues to rise, she enlists the services of the two boys again, and they now stand next to her and hold the signs as she twists and poses and freezes into position, like an electric mannequin, on the roadside by the traffic light.

Two of the boys from the football team have come by and stopped for a photo. One of them holds the phone as the other squeezes a big sponge so that the water pours down her body, and she screams in delight as the photo is clicked into eternity.

Another boy from the school, a senior, scoops her up in his arms for the photo as if he will carry her away, and she takes the picture for him, laughing and kicking her heels in the air.

Even the preacher comes out front for a photo. In it, he kneels before the girl, puts his hands flat together and looks up to her, as if he is praying, or perhaps worshiping.

Then he gets up, flashes the peace sign to the honking passers-by, and walks to the milky-white bucket, where a few others join him to check out the results. As he opens the lid and looks inside, he gets wild-eyed.

Then he raises the plastic bucket up into the heavens and shouts to the members of his congregation, "It's a miracle!".

"And it was so much more *fun* than last year!", Wendy adds.

"It musta' been your brownies", her sister says, and they all burst out laughing again.

As the sun starts to set and the traffic thins, it is clear that the Church of Our Holy Virgin car wash has been a big success this year, and it is all thanks to the sexual exploitation of the under-aged and the unwittingly illegal distribution and consumption of narcotics.

When Jasmine finally relinquishes her throne at the side of the road, her father, Big Jim, comes over to her and wraps a big bath towel around her, to keep her warm.

Then, wiping away a few remaining soap suds, he kisses her on the top of the head.

"Remember, honey", he tells her, "You did this for Jesus".

"I know, Daddy."

At the Donut Shop

Kai Regenbogen steps in front of the doors of the donut shop, and the doors swoosh open for him.

There is again the feeling of too much cold air flooding him from the air conditioning, like when he enters the supermarket and as he sits at his desk at work. Although this mid-summer afternoon is in the middle of a heat wave, this time Kai has brought a sweater along with him.

Once in the shop, the Euro-expat immediately notices a sense of efficiency in everything around him. The workers are polite and friendly to the people they are serving, everybody is standing in line behind one another waiting for their turn, and the workers fluidly and agreeably swivel and stretch and select and unfold and wrap and present everything with a stunning amount of orderliness and kindness – particularly considering that most of them are living painfully close to the poverty line, on one side or another, and that if they pay all their bills this month, some won't even be able to afford to also buy a full box of what they themselves are selling.

In the racks behind the counter, there is an overwhelming assortment of donuts, with different kinds of sugary glazing (pink, light blue, white, marbleized), filling (jelly, cream, pudding), sprinkles (chocolate, orange, emerald green, party-colored), and any possible combination that a person could imagine during that glorious moment when they step up to the counter and say "I want…".

The sheer amount of variety and differentiation that the Americans have put into their production and selection of

116

donuts is amazing. Classical music has its Brahms, Mozart and Stravinsky, and the American donut shops have their "Honey Glazed, Strawberry Cream Dream and Wild Raspberry Swirl".

As Kai wraps his sweater around his shoulders, the young woman in front of him is talking in Spanish on her phone. There is a melodious quality to the language, and Kai is aware of how much more fluid it sounds than his own native German.

In front of her, there is a middle-aged woman, whose pale upper arms display a thickness that testifies to one too many donuts already. The pale woman turns around to the young girl behind her and scolds her.

"Stop blabbering that foreigner talk!", she says bitterly. "This here's America!", and she scowls at the young woman before turning back around to stand quietly, waiting for her turn to buy donuts.

The young woman pauses a moment in her phone dialogue, looks at the back of the other woman's head, and says "Excuse me?" flawlessly, with the modulated and highly pitched voice that is characteristic of Americans.

"This is the United States", the middle-aged woman says, turning half-way around but as though remaining civilly in her place in line. "If you don't like our language, then go back wherever the hell it is ya came from."

With her eyes fixed on the woman in front of her, the young woman says something briefly in Spanish on her phone and then hangs up.

"Who do you think you are, talking to me that way?", the girl says, the light-brown skin of her forehead knit together.

"I'm an American!", the older woman says. "I don't know what *you* are, but we speak English here in America".

The young woman looks back at Kai with her mouth gaping, as if to see if the other people in line can believe what has just happened.

Kai lifts his eyebrows but remains silent.

Then she turns forward again and says, "What I am is a human being, and *who* I am is none of your friggin' business!".

"I'm an American, and it's my business when people don't speak American on line."

"There is no 'American' language. It's called 'English', you fool, and the British brought it with them when *they* moved to this country."

"Well, then speak English if ya know so much about it."

"I'll speak whatever language I choose to!"

The middle-aged woman shakes her head, as if out of some sort of pity for herself, and then she adds calmly, "I wish you people never moved here".

"I *didn't* move here. I was *born* here, lady. My father came here from Puerto Rico and my mother is a Sioux."

"She can't sue *me*. There's fee speech here in *my* country!"

"She's from the Sioux nation, you idiot. That's a tribe of Native Americans."

"Well, yer father shouldn't be filling yer head with all that foreigner talk, if he wants you to live here, like we do."

The young woman juts her head forward in shock.

"Puerto Rico is part of the United States, lady."

The middle-aged woman turns around again, looks at the woman, and then laughs at the nonsense she is sure she has just heard.

"You don't know what yer talkin' 'bout", she says and turns back towards the front of the store.

The young woman steps back and forth in place as she crosses her arms.

"I happen to be studying international economics at the university", she states factually. "If you think that you're so fantastic, may I ask where *your* ancestors come from?"

"My great grandparents moved here from Scotland and the Netherlands a l-o-o-ong time ago, sweetheart, so I'm all American."

"Well, my mother's people were here long before any of your family decided to come here, to what was *our* homeland, before it was robbed from us by foreigners, like you!"

"The Indians didn't own the land. We had a right to come here, too!", the pale-skinned woman says.

The young student laughs.

"Then you shouldn't have any problem with other people coming, like your grandparents did."

"Oh!", the older woman says to the other, as if repulsed by the lack of logic. "That's not the same thing, and you know it!"

"It's *exactly* the same thing – except that my mother's people were here first, before yours even *knew* about this place", the young woman says as she waves her hand, to include the donuts, the seating area, and everything else in the country, from sea to shining sea.

Kai has by now summoned enough courage and he clears his throat.

"Exkoos me", he says to the older woman, "America has *alvays* been a country of people coming vrom somevere else."

She whips her corpulent torso around at the sound of his voice, and she scowls at him as she looks him up and down, with her arms crossed.

"Where are *you* from, now?", she demands of him.

Repeating his frequently required phrase, he informs her calmly, "I am from Chermany".

"Germany?!", the pale woman says, as if shocked and appalled. Then she says, "Well, *you're* OK, I guess. You're here legal", even though the other woman she has been arguing with is a native-born American citizen, and there-fore not an illegal immigrant.

"You people in Germany have been quiet since we gave you democracy", the middle-aged woman adds.

The international economics student turns to Kai and says, "Don't bother trying to talk any sense into her. It's no use".

The worker at the counter suddenly calls out, "Hello, and welcome to 'Go Nuts for Donuts'. How may I help you today, Ma'am?".

"Finally!", the first woman shouts in exasperation, as if she is now also angry with the store clerk, or the donut store, or whatever else it might be. She steps up to the counter and orders a dozen donuts, with an extra one to eat on the way.

As he stands there in line, Kai looks at the towering racks of baked goods for sale.

'And all the different kinds of donuts on the shelves seem to be getting along with each other so well', he says to himself.

The Gun Range

Big Jim's sports utility vehicle shakes and buckles over the uneven dirt road that leads from the gate to the shooting area of the gun range.

Kai is in the back seat with the two teenagers; Big Jim is driving and Wendy is in the passenger seat.

As they turn a corner, they pull up next to a few other SUV's in front of the "Snack 'n Go" snack shop. Jim yanks the gear shift up into the "Park" position, as if he is about to rip if off, and Kai bucks up into the air, banging his head against the hard ceiling.

As Jim shuts off the engine, he turns around suddenly to the Euro-expat and says, with a look of grim seriousness, "Are you ready to rock?".

Rubbing the crown of his head, Kai says, "Yes, I am ready now to rock".

Big Jim stares at him, as if to make sure that his guest is, in fact, duly prepared to rock.

Then Jim says "Let's do it", and he throws his door open and climbs out, casting a quick look first to the left, and then to the right, as if on the watch for invaders.

The other guys are already there – Jim's brother-in-law and most of the other men he had invited to the Barbeque. His brother Alex had already left for home some time ago (the visit was cut short – there was an altercation). Kai was relieved when he found out that Alex would not be joining them at the shooting range with a weapon in his hand.

The family greets everybody, and Kai sees that everyone else – the men as well as the women – are all dressed in camouflage (Jasmine has managed to pull it off so that she looks like a cross between a Cuban guerilla fighter and an angry rap star). The German engineer is suddenly aware of feeling out of place in his white, button-down, collared shirt.

Then the men split up into their group and the women split up into their group, with Bart running and Jasmine strutting into the snack shop for a couple of energy drinks.

The other guys had already started painting their faces with black grease. One of the men rubs two finger tips from one side to the other just below his eye, and a thick, black bar appears.

"Is that make-up?", Kai asks.

The men stop and stare at him firmly.

"It's camouflage paint", one of them states, still staring at Kai.

Their mood seems to be different here today than at the barbecue. They have the attitude that they are about to take care of some very serious business that only men can handle (in spite of their wives giggling together across the dirt path), and that this is no time or place for childish things (even though they have all brought their kids along).

"What purpose does the paint serve?", the Euro-expat asks.

"It's to block the reflection of the sun from your cheek-bones, so you can see, sharp and clear", the man says, looking at his own upraised index finger as he places it at the bridge of his nose and moves it straight out in front of his face, following it with his eyes as if it is his prey.

"It also helps ya ta blend into your deployment surroundings, in case there are any eyes out there, watchin'",
another man says, pointing to the bushes growing behind
the snack shop.

Kai looks at the bushes, to see if anybody happens to be
peering out from them, but there is no one there.

"Try some", the first guy says, holding out to Kai a little
flat, circular container with the black grease, like what Kai
uses to polish his shoes.

Tentatively, Kai dips the tip of his index finger into the
black jar. Then, he applies it in one swirling circle on one
cheek, and then the other, and then he quickly pokes a big,
greasy dot onto the tip of his nose.

He looks like an evil clown.

The man who offered him the grease looks at his buddies and, taking the jar back, says, "Well, I guess that's OK,
for Europe".

Then, the unloading of the weapons begins. The hatch-
backs are lifted high and a tremendous arsenal is taken out
of the SUV's. The men drape themselves with belt after
belt of ammunition, as if preparing for war, and as if they
might not make it back to the SUV (or the snack shop) for
reinforcements, once they head in.

The women do the same, draping themselves as deli-
cately with the ammunition belts as they would with neck-
laces.

As she is taking her AK-47 out from the hatchback,
Wendy pulls her hand back suddenly and looks at her
finger.

"Ow…", she pouts, "I think I just broke a nail!".

124

After the teenagers walk back from the snack shop with their energy drinks (Bart has already gulped half of his on the way), everybody pairs up here and there and takes selfies with each other, in their camouflage outfits, amo and grease paint, holding their weapons. There are pictures of just the guys, just the women, then family shots, and then one big group photo (again, with everyone taking their own selfie of the same pose).

It's a big day, and there needs to be ample footage to document it, before the weekend-warriors all go back to their respective offices or take the kids to school on Monday morning.

There is a lot of military terminology bandied about. Big Jim tells the group that after they "vacate the vehicles", they'll "head in" to the "firing zone", and after a few rounds, they'll all "reconnoiter" at the Snack 'n Go.

Once the strategy has been conveyed, Big Jim says "OK, looks like we're all locked and loaded and ready to go". Then, he raises his hand with the automatic rifle, looks upwards to the sky, and says, "God, make our eyes sharp and our hands steady on this day. And praise Jesus."

And the others answer with a mumbled "Amen".

"OK… BREAK!!", Jim shouts, mixing up his military and his sports jargon.

In separating from the group, Jim's brother-in-law hugs his rifle to his chest and then swirls around in a circle, like a football player avoiding a tackle – except that he ends up in exactly the same place where he was, and then he walks with everyone else a few feet away to the shooting areas across from the targets.

125

As they take their places in the firing lanes across from their individual targets, they each site their guns, and then there is an eruption of sound and a blaze of smoking fire-power, a rattle and roar of discordant explosions and landed shots, from the various weapons that are fired: the AK 47's, the semi-automatic rifles, the machine guns, and a couple of other weapons that normally aren't seen away from military battlefields.

As the men and women shoot, there is a look of intense, crazed hatred in their eyes. Kai sees Wendy scowling fiercely as she lets off a round, and he wonders who she is imagining to be the target of her fury as she shreds the bullseye at the end of her lane.

Big Jim, the friendly host who welcomed him with such a warm, all-encompassing smile into the family's great room, is now raising his upper lip in a kind of snarl, and showing teeth; he looks like a maniacal killer that is enjoying the plunge of the bullets into the flesh of his victim.

This look in the eyes and faces of the shooters is something that Kai does not remember having seen when he visited the local shooting club with his uncle so many years ago, back in his hometown of Rucklingsdorf, Germany. There, they were interested in precision, accuracy, personal skill and accomplishment. They wanted to see who amongst them was the best marksman in town – they did not revel in total annihilation and mayhem like this, not since the war.

Jim steps back from his shooting stance, and Kai notices him making the sign of the cross quietly to himself. Then,

Jim walks a few lanes over to where his son Bart is shooting.

"Show 'em what ya' got, son", Jim says to his boy, with a fatherly smile.

Bart raises his automatic rifle and shoots a wild circle of bullets that land here and there on either side of the target. As he finishes, the upper right edge of the target has been shredded.

The teenager looks up to his father with a questioning look, and Jim rubs his head bruskly, mussing up his hair and pressing his son's head down a bit as he does so, like he does with the family pet.

"Good boy, Bart. *GOOD* boy!", Jim says.

Then Jim looks down the row to his daughter Jasmine. He sees her raising and holding her semi-automatic rifle in different postures, as if replicating pose after pose from various action movie posters she has seen.

He decides to leave her alone, and he comes instead over to Kai, who has been standing behind the row of the others, hands empty, as they shoot.

Jim pauses as he looks at the black swirls of grease paint on Kai's cheeks and the polka-dot on the tip of his nose.

"Anyway", Jim says, as if he has just had a thought that he has chosen not to express, "how 'bout lettin' off a coupla rounds?".

"Oh", Kai says, a bit surprised that his moment has come. "I do not know. Do you sink it vill be OK?"

"Su-u-u-re", Jim says, stuffing the machine gun in Kai's right hand.

They walk to the lane where Jim had been standing.

"Just step right up here", he says, like a carnival barker, and he helps Kai position the machine gun.

"Get a good, firm grip, site your target… and have a good time, dude," Jim says, stepping away, a little farther than usual.

Kai pulls his right index finger slowly, slowly, and nothing happens. He feels like he has already pulled it a tremendous distance, although he has barely moved it at all.

"I do not know if it…" Kai says, and as he pulls his finger further, the trigger makes contact, and the machine gun erupts with a stream of fire and a sharp "Pa-Pa-Pa-Pa-Pa-Pa-Pa…".

The kickback of the weapon throws Kai off balance, the barrel of the gun raises up into the air, and still there is the "Pa-Pa-Pa-Pa-Pa-Pa-Pa". Kai tries to offset the force of the weapon by pulling the machine gun to the side, but he goes too far, and he riddles bullets to the right, and then again far to the left. In his panic, he clenches his fingers and tightens his grasp on the trigger, and he releases barrage after barrage into the sky, back and forth, as if he is trying to murder a rainbow.

As the round of ammunition is expended, the thick grey smoke that surrounds Kai starts to clear, and as he looks around, he is glad to see that everybody is still standing – they are all looking at him, without any doubt, but they are all standing.

There have been no casualties, except for the sign above the "Snack 'n Go" snack shop, which now just reads "ack n' Go", as if the "Sn" had been chewed off in a feeding frenzy.

Jim has his arms crossed in front of his chest, and he is just staring at his "Company Buddy" who had been provided to him at work.

Kai looks back at Jim, and then takes another look around at the environs of the shooting range.

"Did I at least hit the target?", he asks, with a tone of deep, deep apology.

"Nope!", Jim blurts out. "Ya' missed em, dude."

"I missed?"

"Every, single, one", Jim says, and he reaches cautiously to the machine gun and removes it from Kai's hands, as if he is disarming a lunatic during a shooting spree.

After a while, everyone goes back to their shooting at their targets, and Kai heads to the "ack n' Go", alone, for a cup of coffee to settle his nerves.

After an hour or so, the various shooters start to leave their places and head for the snack shop. They order drinks and burgers and then sit at the wooden picnic tables outside and make an afternoon of it.

As the event comes to a close and everyone starts to stand up and clear away their paper plates and food cartons, Jim heads quickly into the snack shop.

When he comes out, he calls "Hey, buddy!", in Kai's direction. As he reaches Kai, Jim turns to the others who are standing around the picnic benches and says, "It is my honor to bestow upon Kai Ray-Gun-Broken this ribbon for Target Range Participation!".

And everybody cheers, whistles and claps as they smile at Kai appreciatively.

129

As Jim pins the ribbon on his chest, Kai says, "But I almost killed everybody!".

Then the man who had handed him the black grease paint earlier says "Buy you came here, dude, and that's what counts."

Kai looks at him.

"Really?"

The man nods. "It's a lot better than those *pansy LIBERALS*, who don't support shootin' and stuff."

There are a lot of quiet, affirmative nods among the crowd, and a few shared grumbles.

"Well, sank you, everybody. Dat is very kind of you", Kai says.

He smiles as he looks at the blue ribbon on his chest, proud to have been recognized in this, his new country, his new home.

He is already planning to hang the ribbon next to his diploma from the German Technical University.

At the Gym

Maybe it was the donuts, or Wendy's cookies, or the endless cake parties at the office, or the... anyway, after a few weeks in America, Kai has noticed that his stomach has started to first protrude, and then head distinctly downwards.

Deciding to take the initiative before things get too out of hand, he decides to spend some time at the local gym, which is in the strip mall not far from his turn onto the main road.

As he opens the door, there is an electronic "Ping!" sound (to replace what would otherwise be a bell) and, as if on cue, a young woman at the counter looks up at Kai and emits a radiating smile as she says, "Hi! Welcome to Fit Right In!".

She is in her early twenties and has very well-toned arms and shoulders. She is also surprisingly tan, considering that she apparently works indoors all day.

"Are you ready to get fit with us?", she bubbles.

Kai walks up to the counter. "Actually...", he says, and then he starts over with "I mean, Hello. Actually, I would like to 'work it out' and 'pump up some iron' today."

The girl looks at him, perplexed, and then returns to radiating her shining smile upon him, as if tanning him with it.

"Cool!", she chirps. Then, still smiling at Kai with her eyes, she waves her hand at the huge display board behind her, with a hand movement that looks as if it has been mimicked from countless infomercials on television.

"We can offer you our 'Sunshine Package', the 'Down and Dirty' or our *'Rockem' Sockem' Action Pack'"*, the last of which she says as she pretends to shadow box in place behind the counter, before breaking into a brief fit of laughter.

Kai notices that around her eyes, the tan stops and her natural skin-tone begins. Under the surface, she is actually rather yellow.

Looking up at the display board, Kai is first impressed with how well all the information is presented. Everything is in its own category, with headings, bullet points, various eye-catching fonts, and a color scheme that makes it simply a thing of beauty to behold.

He reads the options that are before him: the "Sunshine Package" is just the pool, the "Down and Dirty" includes the pool and the weight room, and the "Rockem' Sockem' Action Pack" includes the pool, the weight room, the sauna and steam room, the tanning beds, as well as a free Super-Smoothie of Kai's choice. They don't actually mention Kai's name on the options menu, but they gladly would have, if the Americans had already invented and marketed some computer program to make that "do-able".

A bit overwhelmed at having to make yet another decision from among the countless options available for his personal consumption, he lets out a sigh.

"Actually", he says as he looks back to the girl (he is surprised to see that she has not stopped smiling the entire time he was looking at the sign). "Actually, I just want to come for one day today, please."

"Oh, OK! No problem!", the young woman burst out, "We'll be glad to welcome you as a visitor! How 'bout I just sign you up for our "Healthy Friends" pass? It's good for the who-o-ole day today!"

As she waits for the German engineer to make a decision, she looks like she can barely wait to talk again, to respond, to react, to run a quick sprint or to do some lunges or jumping jacks… something, anything.

"I guess dat vill be fine", Kai says.

"COOL!", she erupts, her eyes tearing open, and she takes out a form. On it are a lot of cartoon drawings of the topics that are mentioned in the brief sentences of the text: there is an inflatable life-preserver ring with a duck's head where the pool is mentioned, there is a drawing of what looks like a pink tropical drink next to the word "Smoothies!", and then there is a long, dense construct of extremely small, tight legal text, that seems to go on, and on, and on, under which there is a blank line, and that is where Kai is supposed to sign.

"That is a lot of informations, just so I can exercise", Kai says cautiously, worried about exactly what he has to agree to in order to be allowed to use the weights – which, after all, he has to make the effort to lift himself.

"Oh, it's just a form everybody has to sign", she says. "Don't worry 'bout it", as she waves the concern away with her toned fingers.

Kai suddenly imagines himself in front of a judge one day, telling him, "But the semi-tanned woman at the gym told me not to worry 'bout it".

Then, he feels his sprouting belly rubbing against the wall of the counter… and he signs, his right eye twitching as he does so.

"Gr-r-r-EAT!", the woman says, as she slips the form rapidly out from under his barely lifted pen tip. Then, she turns to scrawl something on a little rectangle of paper, and she inserts the card into a little plastic frame that she has pulled out from a carton that is full of them, under the counter. Next to that carton, she reaches into another one that is filled with blue lanyards, picks one up, clicks it onto the plastic frame, folds the lanyard in what is obviously the way her boss informed her she should fold it, and she hands the "Healthy Friends" pass to her brand new customer.

"Here ya' go, friend! Welcome to Fit Right In!", she beams at him. Then, as though the amusement ride is not yet over, she makes a sweeping and overly-conscious gesture of her hand and arm towards the next counter, and says, "Don't forget to try one of our Super Smoothies!".

Kai follows the flow of her gesture, from the tight little mound of her shoulder, along her well-defined biceps and triceps, past her supple wrist, to her evenly tanned index finger, which extends and carries his gaze (as if he is no longer functioning according to his own free will) in the direction of the products that the young sales woman is promoting.

"Yes, I vill", Kai says, wondering if that fine print, to which he is now legally bound, requires him to not forget the Super Smoothies.

134

He smiles to the young woman, who also smiles as she waves rapidly back and forth to him, as if he is now already so far away, on his journey to the smoothies counter just a few feet further on.

At the counter, he sees thick, bright green and red mixtures piled up in tall, wide-mouthed glasses, and the smoothies are adorned with little umbrellas and cherries, as if it is a bar in Tahiti. There is a stunningly muscular behemoth of a man working behind the bar, and countless muscles in his upper arms bulge and pulse as he shakes a mixture in his shiny metal tumbler.

"Hello!", the deeply tanned muscle-man says, before he spreads his lips to display his glaring white, bleached smile for the passing customer. "How 'bout a cool, refreshing smoothie today?!", the man says.

Along with the thick, snowy beverages displayed before him on the counter, there are also various exercise items for sale in the display case: weight belts, gloves, sweat bands, thin wiry headphones, smartphone cases with cartoons of barbells surrounded in burning flames, and so on.

There is also a sign which shows pictures of the types of credit cards that are accepted, and the amount is seemingly endless.

As Kai pauses to take everything in, the weight-lifter gives his shiny metal tumbler another shake, making the ice cubes click, as though this added little distraction is intended to push the potential customer over the edge and make him finally say, "Hell, yea! Gimme one!".

Looking at the tendons in the man's jawbone, the skinny Euro-expat summons his own courage and says, "No sank you. I am not sirsty right now."

Then, as though the weight-lifter's impulse to grab Kai by the neck and scream "Eat it, you scrawny punk!" is subdued by an overlying motivation to be professional and keep his job, the muscleman just says, "OK, dude".

As Kai smiles and walks away, the bumpy giant calls out after him, "They're yummy!", and Kai hears the ice cubes being clinked again in the shaken metal tumbler.

Kai follows the sign that says "Changing Rooms", and he is comforted by the fact that everything is laid out for him so clearly, at just the right time when he will need to know where to go or what to do.

After a few steps, though, he approaches a set of three other, smaller signs that are displayed together. One has the symbol for males (with an arrow pointing to the right), another has the symbol for females (with an arrow pointing to the left), and the last little sign has a symbol which seems to be a combination of the two other symbols, and it has an arrow pointing in both directions.

After standing before the signs for a while, Kai follows the one for males and heads to the changing area.

In the room, he selects an available locker and starts changing into his "workout gear" (as the sign in the store had called it). Everything around him is so fresh and clean, and everybody seems glad to be there.

After the Euro-expat removes his pants and underwear, he stretches into the locker for his swimming trunks, which he plans to wear while he exercises today.

136

As he steps one leg onto the bench for balance, he notices the other men in the locker room looking at him (or rather, at the area of his genitals) as though they are trying simultaneously to look as though they are not looking at all.

Kai greets the man nearest him, who lifts his head up from a surreptitious glance and smiles warmly, returning the greeting with a cordial "Hello", as though he had not been caught peeking.

While changing clothes, the European notices that as the American men remove their underwear or swimming trunks, they each turn away from any direction in which any other man might see his private parts. The man who greeted Kai even wraps a towel around his waist and changes his clothes underneath it.

This is very different than on the nude beaches of northern Germany, where Kai spent his summers as a young man. There, everybody was just completely naked, and they would crouch together as they made sand castles, walk leisurely to the edge of the water for a bath, and everybody was comfortable with it – men, women, grandparents, children. There was even a separate section where people could bring their dogs to the beach – all the dogs were nude, as well, and nobody seemed in the least concerned about this otherwise libertine state of affairs.

Once he is ready, Kai blindly follows the signage that leads him into the exercise room.

The room is moderately full, but there is plenty of equipment available. He looks at the long row of shiny metal and black barbells on the rack. At one end, they look like impaled car tires made of iron, and they are frighten-ingly thick.

All the way at the other end, Kai selects the third set of weights from the row, lifts them, and then puts them back before choosing the ones that are slightly smaller.

As he curls them upwards one at a time, a young man in a wheelchair rolls into the exercise area and approaches the nautilus unit. There is already a man in a bright red shirt using the bench of the unit, and the man in the wheelchair asks very politely, "Excuse me. Do you mind if I use the bench when you're done?"

"Oh! Of course!", the other man says, lowering the weights, jumping up to attention and grabbing his towel behind him.

The man in the wheelchair looks at the bench, and then the man who just vacated it looks at it, too, and says, "Oh! Sorry", and starts to wipe the surface of the bench with his towel briskly.

"Thank you", the man in the wheelchair says as he smiles cordially. The man in the red shirt returns the ges-ture, but with a different kind of smile – one that seems somehow nervous.

Then, the young man in the wheelchair stands up fluid-ly, as if getting up from a seat in a restaurant. He steps over the barbells that are lying on the floor and repositions the pin in the black metal bars of the exercise unit, to in-crease the weight.

He then eases himself into position on the polished bench of the nautilus, and he heaves the stack of metal

138

with ease, causing it to hover in the air for a moment before he lowers it evenly.

As Kai watches the weights slide up and down, the bulky, tanned giant from the smoothies counter enters wearing a tank top and heads to the free weights. He smiles to Kai as he passes him and then heads for the opposite end of the row of barbells, heaving the largest of them as he releases a loud, extended grunt, as if he is a howling, suffering animal.

In his swimming trunks and his brand new T-shirt that says "Ain't no Thing!", Kai finishes up at his end of the weights, sets them carefully and quietly back into their original position, and then walks across the room to where the stationary bicycle is.

As he is about to swing his leg across the seat, the young man rolls up to the bicycle in his wheelchair and says politely to Kai, "Excuse me. Can I use the bike, please?", and the young man smiles, as though he expects the answer to be yes.

Kai stops in mid swing and looks down at him.

"But I am using it", he says.

The young man in the wheelchair looks surprised, and seems somehow to be offended. He looks around the room, and Kai notices that everybody else in the area has slowed down their exercises to look his way.

"I won't take long", the young man adds, as he rolls closer to the bicycle.

"Uhm…", Kai says, flabbergasted at the situation. "I am sorry, sir, but you vill have to vait your turn."

The man in the wheelchair stops and sighs, loudly enough for it to be heard across the room.

Then, the man in the red shirt who had originally been at the nautilus unit strides quickly over to the two men at the bicycle with a troubled look on his face. He comes to a standstill and then flashes an award-winning smile at Kai.

"Hi! Howyadoin' today, look", he says, without waiting to find out exactly how Kai is, in fact, doin', "this gentleman would like to use the stationary bike for a while", as if that explains something that is otherwise plainly obvious.

"But", the German engineer stammers, not used to being this far away from a logical connection of ideas, "but I am here already. I am sorry, but he vill have to vait," and Kai continues to swing his leg across the seat.

He is shocked to feel a firm hand suddenly grab his raised ankle, and he looks behind himself to see the man who just spoke to him holding Kai's leg just above his white tennis shoe.

Without releasing the ankle, the man stretches his face into a tight smile and says, "You don't understand. This gentleman is physically challenged."

Kai stares at the man in the red shirt, and then swings his own leg back from the machine, at which the other man releases his grip and smiles again at Kai.

Kai now summons the cold, even rationality that is unique to his culture.

"If der man is physically challenged", he says, slowly and evenly, glaring a whole into the eyes of his conversant, "den he is not able to use a bicycle."

140

Kai stands in his space on the earth, with a crooked, self-satisfied smile of logical victory.

The American stands firmly in front of Kai, returns his sharp look, and says, "But he *identifies* as physically challenged."

Kai pauses, and then lets out a short laugh.

"Vat?!", he shouts. "Are you crasy?"

At that, he sees other people in the exercise room putting down their equipment one by one and slowly walking closer towards the stationary bicycle. The muscular goliath from the smoothies counter is still heaving and grunting, but he has his head turned in Kai's direction.

In front of Kai, the man in the red shirt strikes a more casual pose and says to him, "Look, I dunno how things are in other parts of the world, but here in America, people are free to decide for themselves how they want to be."

He says it as if they are good friends who have simply had a slight misunderstanding, and that he is more than glad to clear everything up for Kai.

"This person identifies as physically challenged," the man adds, "and so everyone respects his right to be who he wants to be."

The engineer from Europe bristles at this violation of his sense of reason. He looks at the crowd that has by now gathered behind the man in the wheelchair. The people are all nodding their heads slowly in agreement, and some of their arms are crossed in front of them.

"I do not sink dat is very respectful to people who are really handicapped!", Kai says, with a certain degree of passive aggression in his tone.

There are gasps of shock in the crowd, and a few people look away.

"The appropriate term is 'physically challenged', sir", the man in the red shirt says, as if reading from a cue card.

"Oh!", Kai says, turning around in place and looking around him for someone who perceives how irrational this has become. "Dat is laughable."

Then he points a finger to the wheelchair and says to the man in the red shirt, "Dis man is no more challenged in lifting der weights den you or I!".

A woman from the congealed mass of people behind the wheelchair suddenly blurts out "Then he is physically liquid!", to which there are further nods and murmurs of support from the crowd. One man even gives the woman an awkward high-five after she finishes speaking.

"Physically liqvid?", the former student of physics erupts. "Wat does dat even mean?"

"It means", the man in the red shirt says, "that a person can decide for him or herself whether he or she is physical-ly challenged at any one particular moment or not", as if he is stating the obvious, while he recites the jargon that is considered politically acceptable at the moment.

Kai reaches for the elastic waistband of his swimming trunks and adjusts it blatantly while he stares at the pair of eyes in front of him. Then, the European raises his arms with a dramatic slowness, like a bird taking flight, and he inserts his hands into his armpits, creating what, for him and his people, signifies that they have become an un-shakable barrier of iron will and defiance.

There is suddenly a sharp "CLINK!!" across the room, as the smoothie giant lets one of the largest and heaviest of the black, metal barbells drop into place on the iron rack.

Then, the weightlifter turns slowly towards Kai, and stares at him, with his lips stretching to bare his glimmering, white teeth in what only dimly resembles a smile.

He then walks slowly to the group that is surrounding the wheelchair, the various muscles in his thighs swelling and protruding through his tanned skin with every step.

As he joins the group, the bodybuilder raises *his* arms, slowly and evenly, in a precise mirroring of how Kai had raised his moments ago, and the man stands there, his bulbous arms crossed to form the very same impervious barrier that Kai had imagined in his mind when he was crossing his own. As the giant heaves his upper torso, the bulk of his sculpted chest swells visibly above the heads of the other people in the crowd.

Just as slowly as Kai had erected his steadfast barrier, it likewise melts, like butter on a hot summer day.

"Vell", he says, looking around for some sort of graceful exit from his capitulation, "If you people vant to be ridiculous", he says… and his eyes fall upon the chest muscles of the tan smoothie behemoth as they twitch, "dan you can be ridiculous."

He turns and heads for the changing room. "I have besser sings to do!".

He walks through the opening of the doorway, and from the safety of the other room, he can hear a roar of celebratory clapping, along with an extended, mass "YA-

A-A-AY!" and a few "WHOO-WHOO-WHOO'S" from the jubilant mob.

Kai shakes his head and looks down at his shiny, white tennis shoes.

'To me, they identify as lunatics.'

The Techno-God

After another exhausting day of impromptu hugging, "I love you's" from total strangers and the general intensity of day-to-day life in America, Kai Regenbogen settles himself wearily into the easy chair in his apartment to watch the news.

The chair is like a gigantic womb, with cushioned areas in places that he didn't even know he had body parts. He pulls the lever on the side and the chair extends soundlessly into the shape of a foamy wave, and he is forced into more of a reclining position than he wants to be in. He has to lift his head from the chair in order to see the television screen, and it soon becomes uncomfortable.

After a few minutes, he tries to evacuate himself from the chair, and the procedure is rather like an upturned turtle trying to flip itself – his legs flounder about in the air as they try to take hold of stable ground, until he finally manages to roll himself over the armrest and onto the floor.

"I do not know why they call it an easy chair", the European expat murmurs into the apartment as he gets up from the floor. "It is not very easy".

He rubs his sore neck and goes into the kitchen. When he returns, he positions the kitchen chair he has brought with him in between the recliner and the television, and he sits to watch the news.

It's a report about a commemoration ceremony at a university. The guest speaker is that guy from Silicon Valley who just hit the top of the Forbes Ultra-Billionaires list after his start-up went public.

"And so, I would like to present to this year's graduating class, our most honored and esteemed guest… Steve *Sugargate*!!"

The camera pans out to the crowd of university students in their glimmering ceremonial gowns, as they all stand and let loose a spontaneous roar of shouts, hollers and applause.

("More yelling", Kai says to himself, as he rubs his temples).

"Dear *Graduates*!!", the speaker shouts as he throws his arms out towards them, to which there is a resounding "*YA-A-A-A-A-A-A-Y*!!" in response.

"You – are – the *future*!"

"*YA-A-A-A-A-A-A-Y!!*", "*THAT'S RIGHT, STEVE!*", "*GO– GO– GO – GO!*"

"And you – are – *America!!*"

"*W-O-O-O-E-E-H!!*"

The speaker radiates at the reaction from his public, nodding his head up and down as though they have responded exactly as he had intended.

"When I wrote the code for the 'You Liyv' app, I was living in my parent's basement", he says, moving on to his main content. "I was broke, I had just dropped out of Princeton, and I had developed so much debt it could choke a walrus."

There are a few giggles from the crowd as they settle down.

146

"But once I kicked everything into high def, the big boys all started knocking right at my door."

He nods again as he looks into the crowd, confirming his own wonderfulness.

"And now, with my little app, *everybody* can fulfill their dream – their dream of taking a selfie, and having their own three-dimensional image appear right before them on their own phones, in the adventure scenario of their choice!"

He pauses for the whoops and yowls he knew were coming, and then he continues.

"Do ya' wanna go kite surfin' in the tropics?", he calls out.

"*Yea!!*", the crowd shouts on cue.

He leans out over the podium.

"Do ya' wanna go rock climbin' in a snow storm?!"

"*YEA!!*"

"Do ya' wanna go street fightin'? Do ya' wanna go ta' *WAR?!*"

"*YEA-A-A-A-A!!!*"

"Well, just download the 'You Liyv' app, and it's all yours -- *your* hologram in an adventure setting of *your* choice!"

The crowd applauds, and then he waves his hand in the air, looks down at the ground and says, "No, wait. Scratch that... *You're* not gonna download the 'You Liyv' app."

There are grumbles and moans of disappointment in the audience at the sudden downturn in the speaker's optimism.

"That's right. Because you don't *have* to."

And the crowd starts to perk back up, stimulated by the excitement of the confusion, and enjoying having just been played.

"Thanks to a little help from the provost office and the university registrar, we have accessed all of your phone numbers and have automatically uploaded the 'You Liyv' app to your phones *right now*, while you've been sitting here!"

And there is a disorderly ruckus as the audience members gape and gasp, pull out their phones and start clicking and swiping, frantically and desperately, like Morse code operators being bombed on the front lines.

As the latest round of American scholars realize the great gift that has been bestowed upon them from the giants of Silicon Valley, they shout and scream and raise their shaking fists into the air, clutching their phones.

And then there is the selfie taking, and the importing of the selfies into the app, and…

"…And that's just the *latest* innovation to come out of the Valley. Every day, we're changing the world. Every day, we're making the world closer, sharper, faster… more fun in every way!"

The speaker has not mentioned the fact that computer technology has limited their own chances of getting jobs, after putting most of their parents out of work or sidelining them professionally. He doesn't say that social networks have estranged them all from each other and made them socially graceless, or that their smartphones have shortened their attention spans to that of fruit flies.

"Yes, we at Silicon Valley have changed the world – and YOU can TOO! You might succeed, you might fail, but that's OK!", shouts the multi-billionaire to the graduating students, who are as-of-yet not gainfully employed and who have already accumulated mountains of debt from their student loans, just so they can be there and listen to him and his version of the modern California sermon.

As he comes to the end of his commencement speech, Steve Sugargate, the latest American Techno-God, looks out into the bright sunshine in which he is basking on this beautiful summer day, and he inhales deeply for his great finale.

"The important thing", he shouts, "is to go out there, and DO something *GREAT*, and CHANGE the *WORLD!!*"

And he closes his eyes and looks upwards as he throws his open hands up into the heavens, in an overwhelming burst of technological ecstasy and optimism, and he smiles a great smile of victory, of success, of unbridled spirit, of being the unstoppable force that he knows he is in the history of modern human progress.

He had expected a wild roar of support and jubilation at this point, but instead – there is silence. With his eyes still closed, he hears only the slight rustling of the leaves of the great oak tree nearby, and there at the podium, in his glorious moment, he suddenly feels briefly naked and alone.

As he lowers his head and opens his eyes, he looks out onto the audience – his people, his America – and the members of the graduating class, in their regal purple gowns, all have their heads bowed down, staring silently at the images of themselves on their phone screens, as they click and swipe, ignoring him and his existence complete-ly, as if he were never there.

From the kitchen chair in the living room, Kai frowns at the television. Then there is a zap of color as he clicks the remote control, and the screen goes blank.

'Yes', the European expat says to himself, 'zat is *much* better now.'

All You Can Eat!

It's been a while, so Big Jim Macintyre thought it would be a good idea to call up his "Company Buddy" and invite him out for lunch. After all, if the Human Resources department were to hear that things had been flagging off a bit, they might reassign Kai to a new "Company Buddy" (and with it, perhaps a few very helpful smiley faces in Jim's company profile, which can make all the difference during his "Employee Review" at the end of the fiscal year).

On the sign that towers over the restaurant in the strip mall, there is a cartoon picture of a scowling horse with bulging eyeballs and sharp, black eyebrows in the angry shape of a hairy "V". The horse is bucking wildly, and above him are the words "Casey's Corral – All You Can Eat!".

'Very appetizing', Kai thinks to himself, as he feels the palm of Jim's hand on his back, pushing him lightly through the door.

They choose a table, and before there is time for any conversation, a waitress bounces up and appears at the side of the table.

"Hi! I'm Suzie!", she bubbles, as she plops two glasses of water down on the table and distributes the menus with a tickled-pink smile.

"Hi, Suzi", Jim says to her, as though they are warm family friends whose history goes back ages.

"Know what ya' want yet, guys?", Suzi the wonderful waitress asks.

"I vill take a minute, please", Kai says, as he smiles to her.

"'*Kay*", she blurts out, and then spins around and darts off into the belly of the restaurant.

"Do you know her?", Kai asks.

"No, she's new here. Never met her before."

The expat looks at the menu, which is full of cartoons and drawings. He reads to himself the names of the dishes: there is the "Super-Saucy Salad", the "Hombre Burger", the "Flame-Thrower Hot Wings" and a number of other items.

"The buffet's really good!", Jim says, looking over Kai's shoulder at the long table of chafing dishes.

Not used to having to wait this long once he has entered such a restaurant, Jim prods a little.

"Whaddaya say, two buffets?", he asks.

Kai looks up, closes the menu and says, "OK, yes. Two buffets".

Jim stretches his head high, back and forth, trying to make eye contact with Suzi the waitress so she can take their orders and they can get on to the matter at hand.

As Kai takes a sip of the water in front of him, his eyes and lips purse together, like he has just eaten a lemon.

"Wassamatta?", says Big Jim.

"Dis vatter", says the expat. "It tastes like pool vatter."

Big Jim tastes his (he is not accustomed to drinking water in restaurants – or elsewhere, for that matter. He sticks purely to either sweetened carbonated beverages or alcohol).

152

When Jim lowers his glass, he looks up and to the side, and then says "Oh, that's just the flouride. They put it in their for people's teeth."

His Company Buddy looks at him, perplexed.

"Don't they do that over there in Europe?", Jim asks.

"No", Kai says – he says it with a tone that means "No, of course not."

"Well", Big Jim says, leaning his elbows on the table and looking indistinctly around the restaurant, "Americans have really good teeth."

With a look of confusion, the European then says, "We have good teeth, too."

"Not like the British, with those black spots?", Jim asks.

Kai lowers his eyebrows, "No, no black spots."

"There, you see?", Big Jim says, apparently satisfied with his side of the discussion for some reason.

The glass starts to feel very cold in Kai's hand. The water is filled with a deep layer of chunky ice cubes, and between that and the air conditioning, Kai's bones and joints are starting to chill. He is suddenly aware that he had forgotten his sweater. It is the middle of a blazing summer, and the need to protect himself from the cold just didn't enter his mind.

Jim raises his eyebrows and smiles to someone behind Kai, and in a matter of moments, the waitress bounces back up to the side of the table.

"So watcha havin' taday?", she says.

She is very friendly, but Kai winces a little at the American's apparent inability to pronounce their own language.

Suzi is standing there alert and ready, with an electronic device in her hand, like the one used to scan for weapons at the airport.

"We'll take two Big Bronco Buffets, Suzi", Jim says, personalizing the order with her first name in order to deepen their friendly relationship. "Oh, and two Cola Chillers, super sized."

The waitress taps the orders into her device, sings "*Got it!*", with her head tossed up and to the side with a big smile, and after Jim's "Thanks, Suzi", she bounces back away, like a happy kangaroo on a pogo stick.

Big Jim "*SLAPS!*" his hands together, and then he rubs his palms back and forth, as if he's trying to start a fire.

"OK!", he says, staring wide-eyed at his dining partner, "let's go in".

He walks ahead to the buffet table at a quick pace, and Kai follows slowly behind.

Jim takes a plate, which he piles with spicy rice, two tacos and a couple of miniature burritos. Then, he dips the tip of the big, metal serving spoon deeply into the chili con carne, scooping up as much as can be leveraged. Long strands of melted cheese stretch up from the chafing dish and follow the spoon, and Jim tugs at the cheese with a pair of tongs he has found, trying to break the strands as much in his favor as possible, without losing in the process anything that he has claimed as being his rightful share.

The chili is poured onto the side of the plate; to make room, the burritos are pressed with the spoon up against the tacos, and all of them are smashed into the spicy red rice, making the rice elevate upwards into a mound. For

154

some reason, even though there is a Mexican theme to the restaurant, there are also French fries available, and Jim scatters a tong-full of them over his heaping, culinary monument.

Following behind, Kai takes a baked potato, one taco and a tuft of salad.

As the two head back to the table, Jim is carrying his heavily laden plate with both hands, watching it carefully and trying to keep it balanced, making sure that nothing falls off onto the floor.

He smiles as he lands the plate successfully on the table, and as he sits, there is a look on his face of total elation. No human being seems more to feel that he is in the right place at the right time than an American does as he sits down to his own heavily piled plate of food at an all-you-can-eat buffet.

As Kai starts to cut a slice of his baked potato, Jim reaches into his pocket with his right hand and, with his left still working the forkful of spicy rice into his mouth, he stretches his phone as far as possible to the side of the table and takes a picture of the two of them eating in the restaurant (perhaps as evidence for Human Resources, just in case).

As they eat, there is a lot of movement noticeable at the tables, with everyone finishing their platefuls of food within a matter of five or ten minutes before going back to the buffet for more. As Kai is finishing his baked potato, Jim has just returned with his third plateful, which towers no less than the two platefuls before it.

Suzi the waitress pops by from time to time to take the soiled plates from the table. As Kai is eating his salad, she says "Are ya' still workin' on that?".

Kai looks at his salad, and then smiles to her and says, "Yes, I am still performing der verk on my salad, Suzi".

She smiles and then goes over to the table across from them that has just been vacated, and she starts to clear everything away at a feverish pace. As she rummages around with the empty plates, cutlery and glassware, there is a hectic sound of glasses pinging and dished clinking together as she piles them up on her little circular tray. Everything happens so quickly and with such purpose and efficiency that it is reminiscent of a big tent being dismantled as a circus prepares to leave town overnight.

As the European expat takes a bite of his taco and chews it several times, he watches his American dining partner hunch over the plate in front of him and scoop food into his mouth one forkful after the next, as though he is trying to perform the act as quickly and as frequently as possible in a given time.

Pausing suddenly, still with his own head close down to his plate, his fist wrapped around his fork and his arm raised at the shoulder, Jim looks at the way Kai is eating.

"Wassamatta?", Jim says, "Isn't yours any good?"

"It's fine, Jim", Kai says. He can't really notice much more than the two basic flavors of salt and sugar in what he is eating, but he doesn't see any reason to mention that just now.

As Big Jim continues to feed, Kai looks around the room at his surroundings. He notices that nearly everybody is overweight: the men, the women, even the kids. The children have already gone past that shape of Michelangelo angel fat all the way to early obesity.

Generally, everybody else in the restaurant is eating the way Big Jim eats. As Kai sits upright and eats his food one small forkful at a time, he notices that people are shoving their chairs back noisily and abruptly the moment they finish – like race horses let loose from their stalls – and heading back to the buffet table for seconds or thirds. They are generally wearing shorts that come down to their thighs, and their shirts are hanging out of their pants, curving over the upper surface of their bellies and then cascading helplessly into a freefall, where the cloth just dangles haphazardly, a foot or more removed from their actual waists.

They mostly walk with a distinctly backward-leaning incline and with their feet spread outwards at the toes, as if they are waddling like plump penguins to a feeding hole.

At one table across the room, there is a family of four. The children are rocking back and forth in their chairs, like asylum patients, and there is a constant, ongoing begging and whining by one child about ice cream. The buffet is out of his favorite flavor, so the mother tells him to try whatever is there. The boy climbs down the chair, goes to the buffet table and brings a scoop of the other flavor of ice cream in a little silver dish. Back at the table, he tastes the emergency flavor and doesn't like it, and so he returns to wining loudly and complaining.

As Kai is finishing his lunch, a balled-up napkin is launched from the child's table and lands on the rug next to Kai's leather loafers.

Jim is slowing down over his second plateful of fried bananas, flan and two kinds of ice cream. He looks sleepy, as though he regrets what he has just done to himself.

Finishing the last spoonful of ice cream, he pushes the plate away from himself slowly, as if he never wants to see it again. Then, his eyes wide, he breathes in deeply and puffs his cheeks up with the air, which he lets out in a thin stream through his pursed lips, the way alcoholics tend to do.

"Are you OK, Jim?", Kai asks him. "You look like you are going to be sick."

After another deep breath, Jim says, "Yea, I'm OK, buddy", and he winks his eye. "You ready to take a spin by the Ice Cream Shaq?"

Close One

"And in other news, there's been a shooting at a Junior High School in…"

Kai stops shining his shoes and darts his head out the bathroom doorway to see the television screen.

"Oh, no. Not another one", he says to the screen, his eyes fixed on the images that are playing out in front of him, his brush held motionlessly in one hand and his right shoe in the other.

As he is following the events, the same news program is being viewed in thousands of other homes and businesses across the country, including in one particular office, which is located on a top floor in one particular skyscraper that towers over a major American city.

A flat monitor is recessed seamlessly into the wall of the office, and the monitor's reflection can be seen in the surface of the giant, polished mahogany table in the center of the room. Around the table are several black swivel chairs, and the people in the chairs are wearing business suits of the highest caliber.

"They're gonna be at our *throats* this time, Bill", one of the executives says to the man who is pacing back and forth at the head of the table. "We barely held them off with the last one."

"I know… I know!", the other man says. "We gotta think of a way to turn this thing around, somehow."

"Whadda ya' mean, turn it around? It's a shooting, and this is the United Association of Firearms Organizations!"

"Yea", a woman at the table adds, tapping the tip of her pen repeatedly into a notepad on the mahogany surface. "We've already been gettin' more calls from Washington after that last one in Nevada. The heat's pickin' up."

"OK, OK!", the man at the head of the room says, raising the palm of one hand to the others as he continues pacing, his other hand cradling his forehead. "But there's gotta be some way to spin this thing, so that it lands in our favor..."

The voice of the newscaster continues in the background from the monitor.

"… and the victims have been identified as…", the reporter's voice drones on, as pictures of one teenager after another start to appear on the screen.

"Wait! I got it!", the President of the UAFO shouts as he throws both hands up beside his head. His eyes are gleaming, as if the discovery is burning from inside of him. As he looks at the other executives silently, he has a tight, uncontrollable grin, as if he is relishing the expression that will be on their faces when he unveils his brainstorm to them.

"…and Miranda Gilcrest, who was just entering the cafeteria when the…", the reporter says, as the photo of a smiling 14-year-old girl in a shirt with a picture of a big sunflower on it appears on the screen.

In the photo, the girl has her arm around another girl, her best friend. The picture was taken when the two girls were at the state fair a month-and-a-half ago. Miranda had put on her favorite shirt with the sunflower, because she was glad that she was going to spend the day with her friend on the amusement rides. When she took out that shirt, she didn't know that it was the way everybody in the country was going to see her on the news after her being murdered in the cafeteria in school. She didn't know that was the shirt that was going to be in the photograph that her parents would be staring at 10, 20 years later, as the memory of her started to fade against their will, as they tried to fight against that fading with everything they had inside of them, by trying to keep the memory of her fresh and alive, by looking at that picture, the one of her in the shirt with the big sunflower on it, the shirt that she took so casually out of the drawer that day instead of the light blue one with the ruffled shoulders, which she almost chose instead.

"What is it?!", a man in thin, wire-framed glasses and a grey suit says from one of the swivel chairs.

The president of the association continues smiling, and then he slowly utters the two, distinct words "safety...cages", as if it is the punch line of a macabre joke in his own head, and as if he himself can barely believe the simplicity of his own brilliant discovery.

"Whattaya mean, safety cages?", the woman says, leaning with her elbows onto the mahogany table.

"*Martin Croft, 14 years old*", the reporter's voice drones, as the next photo in blended in place of the one before.

"Safety cages!", the Association President repeats, throwing his hands up into the air and shrugging his shoulders, as if it's obvious now. "We'll sell the schools cages that teachers can keep their guns locked up in at school."

"*Maryanne Watson, who had just celebrated her 13th birthday last week*", the reporter says, as a picture of a smiling young girl opening a gift-wrapped box is flashed on the screen.

"We'll get the production contracts through our metal processing companies. We're gonna make a *fortune!*"

The woman at the table looks up at the screen, and she abruptly stops tapping her pen.

"There're all scared! They need to feel safe, so we'll sell 'em safety!", the president says, almost giddy with the potential of his idea.

The man in the grey suit looks at the woman's face, and then at the screen. Then, he lowers his head and sees the boy's face in the reflection of the rich, mahogany table.

"Safety cages. No, wait, wait… *FREEDOM* cages!", the man at the front of the room shouts, throwing his arms wide open in his own ecstasy.

He looks at the half dozen faces in the room, and they all start to melt, looking down and away from him.

"What?", he says to them.

"*…and John Abercromby*", the reporter's voice continues, as the boy's photograph glares on the monitor that is recessed so seamlessly into the office wall, "*son of William F. Abercromby, President of the United Association of Firearms Organizations…*"

Barking in the Night

As the orange fades from the sky and turns into a dark blue, on its way to black, there is the deep, rhythmic sound of a large dog barking.

"WOWF. WOWF. WOWF".

Big Jim is sitting on the couch watching TV next to the open window to the back yard. He has his remote control in his hand, his arm is draped over the side of the sofa, and a super-sized bag of Low-Carb Party Chips is cradled to the side of his lap.

"WOWF. WOWF…WOWF".

"Shut up, Rock!", Jim calls, turning halfway to the open window, without letting his eyes leave the T.V. screen.

It's quiet now. There are insects chirping and whirring, and…

"WOWF. WOWF."

In the window of the neighboring house, two fingers and a thumb poke open the venetian blinds and a hidden face peeks out into the darkness.

With his eyes still fixed upon the TV screen, Big Jim hollers from his sofa in the living room, "Rock! I told you to shut up!!".

"WOWF".

"Rock!"

"WOWF!"

"ROCK!"

"WOWF!"

"*ROCK!!*"

The fingers from the neighboring window suddenly slip away and disappear.

Every night, it's like this.

Good Lord

"Yes, I vould *luff* to go to am American church wit you, Jim!"

That was Kai's response when his Company Buddy invited him to come along with his family to mass one Sunday.

Back in Germany, Kai had seen American movies that showed Baptist churches, with everybody calling out spontaneously and singing gospel music, loud and strong. Everybody seemed so happy, so inspired. Their clothes were all festive and colorful, too – the women in their yellow and their emerald green Sunday dresses, the men with their deep royal blue Stetson hats, looking sharp, in their bright cloth suits and their shinny black shoes with the white spats.

It was like nothing Kai had ever seen before. To him, *that* was America, and that was what he was looking forward to when he accepted Jim's invitation.

On Sunday morning, after Big Jim Macintyre has driven the SUV past the shopping centers and the strip malls (with his wife next to him and Kai in the back next to the teenagers, of course), he turns off the main road and follows the curves along the tree-lined street.

Then, there up ahead, Kai sees it: it is a quaint, little wooden church with pleasant architectural flair, painted immaculately in bright white. It looks so graceful and charming, and out front are people just like Kai had seen in all those American movies: the brown-skinned Americans in their bright Sunday attire, gathering and mingling in front of the pretty church building. Everyone seems so polite to each other, seeing each other and being seen, and it looks like one, great party – a party that he has been invited to and of which he will soon be a part.

Kai smiles as the scene grows larger with their approach. As they reach the paved entrance to the churchyard, though, the SUV doesn't slow down to turn (in fact, Jim seems to have stepped on the gas a little), and the church and the colorful hats and the festive people all recede behind Kai, finally disappearing as the SUV continues on around the next turn.

"Exkoos me, Jim. Is dat not your church we just passt?"

Jim looks in the rearview mirror at Kai.

"Oh, no no!", Jim says, chuckling spontaneously, and then looking sideways to his wife Wendy as they share a little smile at their foreign guest's naive misunderstanding.

"That's the black church", Jim adds, as if the matter is thereby settled and no further explanation could possibly be desired by anyone, from either side.

Kai looks at the back of Jim's and Wendy's heads as the SUV continues driving along. Wendy is humming along to the Christian Rock music that is playing on the car radio in the background, and she has a look of easy contentedness as she sits and looks out the windshield.

There is a sharp, metallic rasp of white noise coming from the earphones in each of the kids' ears: from the black one leading out of Bart's ear and the lavender one leading out of Jasmine's.

After they pull up into the parking lot of Jim's church, Wendy shouts, "OK, kids, we're here!!!", loud enough to be heard over the white noise from the back seat, and as though the earphones would somehow have prevented the teenagers from having seen for themselves the fact that they had arrived.

They all get out, and as Bart walks past his mother, she grabs him and starts to poke his dangling shirtfront into the beltline of his jeans.

"This is church now, Bart. Remember, tuck for Jesus."

"Aw, Mah", Bart whines at the child-like handling.

Jim closes his door to the SUV with a slight slam and says with a disinterested, singsong tone, "Listen to your mother, son" while looking in the other direction to spot familiar faces.

As Wendy walks around the front of the SUV to meet her husband, Bart rustles around with his shirt and pulls it back out of his pants before heading off towards a group of other teenage boys.

Jim is wearing a pair of blue trousers with a black belt. The leather around the holes of the belt is imprinted from where the buckle had previously been fastened so many Sundays before. Kai recognizes Jim's outfit from the office. It's clean, and professional – but there is no felt Fedora on his head, as Kai had been expecting.

They walk towards Wendy's sister and her family, and they all chat for a while before heading towards the church building.

At the entrance, the pastor is there to welcome everyone, exchanging a few words as they pass through the doorway. Even though it's Sunday, the preacher is not wearing any religious gowns of any kind. Instead, he is dressed in a tree-piece, navy-blue suit. As he shakes hands with Jim, a gold watch protrudes from the pastor's white shirt cuff. Kai notices that the watch matches the reverend's cufflinks, which in turn match the shiny, gold clip in the preacher's tie.

Greeting Jim's wife, the preacher smiles and says, "Did you bring any of those wonderful brownies today, Wendy?".

"Oh, Father", Wendy says, as she looks away and giggles. She raises her hand to give the preacher a playful little slap, like she would to Jim when they are joking, but then she stops, remembering suddenly that the reverend is a man of the cloth.

The members of the congregation shuffle into the building to their places in the wooden benches, and as the organ music from the back begins, there are a few coughs and a general change of body posture, with people wriggling into their places and sitting more upright.

The preacher enters from beside the altar, but he has now adorned himself in a robe, through which his navy-blue suit is still visible at the upper chest and wrists.

The various rituals of the mass are conducted, and it doesn't take long for the posture of the congregation members to return to where it had been before, and then go long past that into a generally inattentive slump.

The priest folds up a long strip of embellished cloth, which he kisses before he places it upon the altar behind him, and then he steps to the pulpit to deliver this Sunday's sermon.

"Dear brothers and sisters", he begins, as he floods the congregation with a warm, all-encompassing smile, "we are gathered here today to celebrate the great work of our Lord, and to thank Him for the prosperity that He has bestowed upon us, as the fruits of our labor."

There are some quiet nods from the members in the wooden benches, but mostly he has already lost them at this early point, out of sheer habit.

"We thank Jesus, for giving us the drive to work hard, to go that extra mile, to take that extra rush to the goal line", he says, making a fist and and raising it slightly, as if he is grasping hold of the air in front of him.

To the left of where Kai is sitting, a man mumbles a weary "Amen", more to himself than anything else. The man's eyes are baggy and he is gazing vaguely into the void in front of himself. He looks like he has not fully slept in weeks.

"It is through our Lord that we gather the strength to put bread on our tables and clothes on the backs of our families, and to enjoy the success and wealth that God allows us in this great country of ours", he says.

Kai looks at a woman sitting a few rows in front of him. She is wearing silver earrings that hang from little chains at her earlobes. Watching the light from the window reflect on the curves of the silver chain links, Kai is not aware that the woman's house just went into foreclosure, and that she bought the earrings with her credit card at 26% interest.

The pastor raises his hands and looks up to the rafters, smiling gratefully, and says to the ceiling, "We are truly blessed!".

In fact, the preacher himself has actually developed a considerable debt, which is now in the hundreds of thousands, but he has managed to hide it so far through various loopholes in the tax code.

"But not everybody is as eager as we are to head to the same goal line", the preacher says, suddenly changing his tone and scowling at the audience. "Not *everybody* is on God's team."

He shakes his head remorsefully and then continues.

"No, my brothers and sisters, there are some who believe that our God is not the real God, who are *against* our God!", he says, and he tightens his grasp onto the wooden framework of the pulpit.

"There are some who believe that only *they* know the path to righteousness, but my brothers and sisters, righteousness is as foreign to them as are the cornerstones of our values, our ethics – our beliefs that have made this country into the shining beacon on the hill that it has been for hundreds of years!"

"Amen", Big Jim says quietly as he frowns from his place in the wooden bench. At this unexpected disturbance so close to him, his son Bart's expression changes from one of vague distraction to guilty alertness; the boy looks at his father, and then faces forwards, scowling as well, and repeats his father's "Amen!", but with an added vigor.

"You will not see those others here in church beside you, oh humble worshipers of the Lord", the preacher adds. "No, you will not see them here... but you *will* see them as they pass by us, on their way to hell."

There are several tired nods of affirmation from the faces of the congregation, as they look off distantly and unfocussed into the void in front of them.

"Ours is a peaceful congregation", the reverend ads, standing a bit further back from the pulpit now, "ours is a forgiving congregation."

He looks about at the heads tilted in different directions before him.

"Why, it isn't long ago that I myself was reminded of how pious a congregation we have amongst us. It isn't so long ago that I was subjugated to evil judgment and false accusations, by those who refuse to believe in the light, and who only want to believe in evil."

The few members in the audience who are still paying attention now start to look away from the alter – at the big crucifix above them, at the sculptures along the walls of the church.

"Why, there were those voices that shouted hateful words like 'theft' and 'plunder', and who did not believe in the greater goal of the "Help Your Brother" program that I was inspired to found, a program which was funded by the generosity of the noble hearts of the members of this very congregation!"

He gazes out at the crowd silently, with a look of challenge in his eyes. Then he nods his head affirmatively.

"But ours is a congregation of peace", he says quietly. "Ours is a congregation of forgiveness. I have opened my heart up to the Lord and asked for the forgiveness of *my*

171

sins", he says, looking innocently upwards at the ceiling – he suddenly notices that the wet mark from last year's storm damage is starting to expand – "and by the grace of God, I was granted this forgiveness."

After a pause, he looks back downwards upon the members of the congregation and adds, "And that is why I have faith that the Lord above us will inspire you, as well, to be more than just a little Christian and to open up your hearts, as well as your purse strings, as the basket is sent around. The 'Help Your Brother' program needs you, and the Church of Our Holy Virgin needs you, as well, to protect itself and its leadership from the snarls and fangs of false accusations and the treachery of unrighteous legal fees."

A few attendants start to appear at the sides of the rows. They pass little wicker baskets into one row of the crowd, and after the baskets make their way through the first row and back along the next, being filled with dollar bills of various denominations, the baskets are collected and sent along into the following row, to be passed further around.

"So open your hearts, my brothers and sisters, and remember – to give, is to forgive."

As the baskets are filled to overflowing and then carried to a dark little room in the back of the church, the preacher performs a few more rituals, and then he turns to the crowd and says, "It is time to offer each other, the sign of peace", and as if a trigger has been pulled for them, everybody turns to the person nearest them and shakes their hands, some with a look of pious dignity, some with a look of kindness and friendliness.

There is even some stretching for some high-five between a couple of guys who are a few rows removed from each other but who know each other rather well. Occasionally, there is the casual handshake that consists of two palms slapping against each other and then sliding away into a clasp of finger tips.

"As you resume the journey of your lives outside", the pastor resumes after everyone has quieted down, "remember to love your brethren, and do not let yourself be infected by the others, who are on the wrong path."

Then the reverend raises his hands poignantly, looks aloft and begins upon his lengthy closing.

"This mass is ended..."

"Amen!!", Kai blurts out uncontrollably – and all the members of the congregation turn to stare at him with an angry, suspicious look, as if they are suddenly wondering whether or not he is on the right team.

Keeping up with the Joneses

"Wend, we got anything ta' eat?!", Jim shouts into the hollow cave of the refrigerator.

Wendy's voice calls out from inside the bedroom. "There's fruit. The doctor said you're saposta eat fruit!"

Jim grimaces into the refrigerator and then closes the door.

As the phone rings, he reaches to the counter and slaps the speaker button of the phone console.

"Hlo", he says.

"Mister Macintyre? We've been trying to reach you. You have a couple of loans with us that have been due for payment for a while, and –"

"Booooooooooooo" the telephone moans after Jim slaps at the disconnect button. Then he slaps again at the speaker phone and the tone is silenced.

Soon, the quiet is disturbed by the sound of a light whir. It is the automatic mechanism of the neighbor's garage door.

Jim looks out the patio door, stretching and craning his neck to see around the laundry that's handing on the line outside.

Out of the opening of the garage, as if through the process of birth, the black metal housing of the neighbor's new lawnmower appears, glimmering in the early sun. It doesn't make the rickety sound of wheels wobbling on the driveway that the neighbor's old lawn mower used to make.

After polishing a smudge from a leaf off of the housing, the neighbor stands back up and returns to his place behind the handle, where there is a shiny silver key sticking out. Jim watches as his neighbor turns the key and the engine turns over and comes to life, as if awakened from a dream.

"Hmm!", Jim grunts to himself. He remembers tugging at the cord of his *own* lawn mower last Saturday. The motor just wouldn't turn over, and he tugged and tugged so hard that his hand slipped off the cord and he knocked a vase over with his elbow; it fell from the mosaic café table he had bought at StuffCo for $ 295. Hurt his shoulder, too, and Wendy wasn't too pleased about the broken vase.

"What's that?", Wendy calls through the open patio door as she enters the great room with a big plastic basket full of dirty laundry. A lock of her hair is hanging loose as she picks up an old sock from the back of the couch and tosses it into the basket.

"Mike got a new mower", Jim says.

"Who?"

"The Jonses next door. Got themselves a new lawn mower."

Wendy sticks her head through the patio doorway and peeks attentively between the sheets hanging on the line.

"Nice one", she says, and then she looks at Jim briefly before going back to the couch and rummaging under the seats for the other dirty sock.

After a lever on the handle is clenched, the mower starts moving on its own. As the neighbor steers it to the front corner of the lawn to start mowing, he catches sight of Jim on the patio.

Jim ducks behind the sheets, but the neighbor stretches his hand up high into the air and waves it in slow, wide movements, back and forth, so Jim stretches up likewise and waves back, smiling and calling to him "Hey, Mike… nice mower!"

Mike waves back again and turns back to his lawn. As he mows, Jim notices that the neighbor is not hunched forward, pushing the machine onwards against its will, like Jim has to do. He's just walking casually behind it as it pulls itself along, looking at the flowers and plants as he goes, as if he's taking the mower out with him for a quiet stroll, like a good friend.

Jim remembers himself trying to maneuver his own rickety gray mower up over that little hill around the trunk of the big tree last weekend. He was sweating pretty heavily, and he must have been complaining to himself because he remembers hearing Wendy say "Do ya' hafta curse so goddam much all the time?!".

As Jim stands there on the patio, the decision is made that there will be not only the equivalent of the neighbor's electric-starting, self-propelled lawn mower in the Mac-intyre yard, but a lawn mower that is even better, greater somehow – though Jim is not exactly clear yet as to the details, or even what it is he is yearning for, exactly. He only knows that there is a yearning – much like the yearning he feels when he goes to the bronco buffet.

Through the open wooden gate at the Joneses' house, there is some structure that Jim can see in the back yard, but he can't make out what it is.

He stretches on the tips of his toes and peers over the sheet hanging from the line, but over the neighbor's fence, he can only see the very top of some object in the yard there.

He looks at the wrought-iron chairs that surround the mosaic café table, and he decides to step tenderly on one for a boost.

He juts up like a bungee cord and then back down to the ground, but not before having seen the new barbeque in Mike Jones' backyard. It was a thing of beauty. So big, with... how was it again? He only caught a fleeting glimpse of it over the fence boards.

He steps his foot back on the chair, and then pulls another of the wrought-iron chairs closer and positions it for his other foot. He then lifts himself up on the first chair and, once aloft, taps with his other foot to find the surface of the second chair, and he balances there, tentatively, like a trained elephant rearing up on its two back feet at the circus.

Crouching and trying to distribute his weight evenly to keep his balance, Big Jim peers over the fence into his neighbor's yard. His eyes widen like those of a child and his mouth gapes as he beholds the largest, most expansive looking barbeque he has ever seen. There is enough space on the grill to roast a wild boar – tusks and all. The cover curves out so fully that, if removed, the most important guests at a party could practically shelter themselves under it in case of rain.

The product makes his current grill look like the most primitive of barbeques, like a barbeque must have looked a hundred and fifty years ago – closer to just a big tub of metal with a fire in it than anything else, rather than anything a successful American can manage to get for himself.

He thinks of the guys when they came over for the grill party a few weeks ago, and he remembers himself manning the grill with such pride and virtuosity. Well, that was another day, another age, and he has never been one to let himself fall behind the times. There are obviously new models on the market now, and one thing he knows is that Big Jim Macintyre isn't going to embarrass himself in front of his friends and family by cooking on a barbeque that isn't top of the line, ultra-modern, a barbeque that is "less than" – after all, a real American like himself needs a real, American barbeque.

The neighbor's barbeque has a graceful form that he has never seen in such an item before. Its cover curves to hug the shape of the cooking area, and the coating on the surface looks so deep, so rich.

Jim finds the neighbor's barbeque alluring, sultry even. It is newer and younger than his own, and it reminds him of a time when *he* was new, and young, when he first started grilling.

Balanced on the two wrought-iron chairs, he recalls those times – and the memory makes him feel free again, powerful, like when he was a young buck, with so much ahead of him, before so many things happened, before –"

178

"Are these your dirty socks in the sofa?!", his wife shouts shrilly from the great room.

As his fantasy is interrupted, Jim takes one last look at the provocative barbeque on the other side of the fence, and then he feels himself tilting slightly off balance. The wrought-iron chair slips from under his right foot, and he topples, clutching at nothing, and tumbles backwards as his head smashes with a loud "THUMP!" against his grimy barbeque.

"Crappy old thing!", he shouts, as he scowls and rubs the back of his head.

"Do ya' always gotta *curse* so friggin' much?!", Wendy shouts, as she rushes away into the laundry room.

Still rubbing his head, Jim rolls onto his side, and then onto all fours. He tries to stand up, and it's like a giant panda bear at the zoo.

Still frowning, he goes to the TV area, picks up his smartphone from the table and taps the Internet icon to go online. At the StuffCo site, he searches for the "Garden" section, and then for "Grills/Barbeques" – and there, at the top of the list under the heading "StuffCo's Best", he sees it: the "Turbo Charge X-5000". It's a beauty, the latest model, with two shiny, golden gas tanks and a separate grill on the side, which can be pulled out through a series of artic-ulated joints, for Jim's added grilling pleasure.

This is his new barbeque. There is no question about it, and the choice seems to be bigger than Jim himself, bigger than the barbeque's spacious grilling surface, bigger even than StuffCo. It is manifest destiny, and he's got to have it.

As Wendy rushes by with a pile of folded bath towels, Jim says to her, "I think I'll buy us a new Barbeque", still looking at the picture on the screen in front of him.

Wendy stops, looks at him, and then clicks her head forward again and continues on into the bedroom at a rapid pace.

He enlists his son, and they both get into the giant SUV and drive across town to the supercenter.

The wide, glass doors of StuffCo open automatically for them and they enter. As Jim looks up, he sees a canoe suspended from the ceiling of the giant warehouse, hanging by cables over the countless racks of shelves. It is an oversized model, with a formed-plastic "Sandwich Chest" installed at the back, but it is nevertheless dwarfed in the spaciousness of the monstrous building.

"This place is great!", Jim says out loud, still staring at the suspended canoe with the added Sandwich Chest.

"Yea", Bart agrees. "It's pretty cool."

They take one of the overly proportioned shopping carts, and in spite of Jim's size, it makes him look small and vulnerable as he pushes it.

Through the airplane-hangar-like building, they pass row upon row of items that they had not thought of buying until seeing them on the shelves there in front of them, just now. As the father and son meander along, sometimes pausing to look at a display and sometimes just reaching out for an item and taking it without stopping as they pass by, they add one box after another into the cart, like children eating one piece of candy after the next until their stomachs hurts.

They finally come to the doors of the garden center, and as the doors whoosh open for them and they pass through, they are instantly in a wide-aisled, well-organized labyrinth of more flowers, plants, bushes and trees than Jim has seen anywhere else in his life. They are all pristinely manicured and grown, and there is a scent of vibrancy and sweet fruitiness in the air. It is like Jim is on an exotic vacation, there in the gardening department of the StuffCo Supercenter in town.

They pass the passion flowers and the other exotic plants, which nobody seems to be able to keep alive once they leave this magical environment of the garden department.

Then, the lion sites his first prey – it is a robotic lawn mower, with a remote-control option. Jim smiles deviously the instant that he sees it, realizing that it is so far beyond a self-propelled lawn mower with an electric starter. Mike Jones won't even stand a chance.

Without thinking, Jim instinctively selects the bright red one from the assortment of boxes (the other choice is a nefarious black model). It's an unconscious decision, based upon a natural awareness that the bright red one will be more noticeable by the Jonses, as well as everybody else in the neighborhood (what the hell, while he's at it).

He smiles to his son as he adds the box to their cart, and they roll onwards to the picnic display. There, in the center of the row of barbeques, Jim instantly recognizes the "Turbo Charge X-5000" that he saw on the Internet. It is peculiar to see his own personal, future possession here, standing exposed amongst these strangers.

He takes a purchase slip from the plastic display holder and they head towards the cashier, adding to the shopping cart as they go: a new barbeque brush, a device with a long metal handle for broiling fish, a full-bodied barbeque apron (with a picture of a pig in a chef's hat standing in front of a barbeque and with a speech bubble that says "Come an git' it!") and, of course, a twenty pack of D-sized batteries – because you can always use those.

He maneuvers his cart like a tug boat into the corral of the cashier lane.

"Hi, welcome to StuffCo!", the cashier says. "Are you having a fantastic shopping experience?!" to which Jim responds, "You bet!".

Meanwhile, his son starts piling candy bars from the impulse rack onto the moving conveyor belt.

Big Jim notices this and starts to scowl; then he looks at the candy rack and quickly adds a "Megabyte" candy bar for himself – plus a package of AAA batteries.

When he swipes his plastic credit card through the slot of the payment unit, he does so with the familiarity and ease of someone who has made the movement countless times before, like a tennis player who is a master of his sport.

"Beep!", the machine goes.

"I'm sorry, sir. Your credit card has been denied", the cashier says, with a look of embarrassment and empathy.

"Oh", Jim says, and he reaches into his back pocket and pulls out his chunky wallet. After unfolding it, he selects another credit card from the six or so that are available (carefully avoiding the blue one with the gold lettering on it), and he flips it out to the cashier with a casual "Here ya' go".

The sale is rung up, the cashier smiles and says, "That's for buying your stuff at StuffCo!" and Jim says, "No problem. Have a good one!".

He and his son walk to the automatic doors, and the doors open as if they are spreading as far as they can and then just a bit more, to make way for the protruding boxes and packages in the cart.

Jim's eyes wince from the shock of being back in the blaring sunlight again, and he and Bart head to their sports utility vehicle.

Bart stands at the trunk, but his father walks to the side of the vehicle and says, "We gotta put all this junk in the back seat", using the term that addicts use to refer to their drugs. Then he adds, "Gotta make room for the X-5000", calling the product by the marketing term, instead of just saying the "barbeque".

Jim and his son mount the vehicle, like cowboys in the Wild West mounting their horses. Then Jim shifts into reverse and guides the steering wheel with his single index finger (power steering, of course). The SUV beeps to identify that there is an object behind them, ensuring Jim that there is one less thing that he has to pay attention to.

Bart looks at the various gauges and meters on the dashboard. The SUV is not really like a car, per se; it is more like a fuselage, with its multiple levers and buttons, recessed displays and glossy surfaces, practically none of which are actually necessary for the act of traveling between two points safely and out of the rain.

Once the vessel has left its port, they head around the side of the building.

There, after they pass a few sandy areas, there is a big sign above a hangar door that reads "Pick Up". Customers have to come here when their purchases are too big to fit in the oversized shopping carts or, in some cases, to fit through the doorway.

Driving home, Jim is having some trouble seeing past his "Turbo Charge X-5000" barbeque in order to see the traffic behind him. The other cars on the road are likewise filled with big boxes, and during the drive, Jim's keen eye is alert for any signs of the standard of consumption that the packages inside and strapped to rooftops of the cars display. After his appraisal, he concludes that he has done well with the X-5000, and he has a sense of accomplishment at his conquest.

He is proud that his son can be there and see him during such a moment, being able to buy the biggest and the best that's available. Jim casts a quick glance at Bart, who has his head down and is clicking mundanely at his smartphone.

"Yes, family", Big Jim thinks to himself, with a swelling sense of pride and satisfaction. "It's all for the kids."

They pull up into the driveway, and Jim and Bart carry the bags and various boxes around back into the yard, including the boxes for the automatic lawn mower and the new barbeque.

On the patio, Jim takes the remote-controlled lawn mower out from the Styrofoam hulls and the plastic bag and looks at it. He turns it over to view it from all sides and he smiles, like a kid at Christmas.

Then he turns to his son and says, "OK, let's do it!", and they smile at each other before Jim rips the pull tab along the cardboard and takes out one separate, little white box of accessories after another.

Then he turns the huge, cardboard rectangle on the side and says "Hold the box", as he slides out the various modules of the barbeque and the shining, golden gas tanks.

"We gotta put it all together", Bart says, daunted at what lies before them.

"Yea", Jim says, looking helplessly at all the parts. "Well, let's just take a look at the instructions, here".

The first few pages are filled with legalese in very small print. Some of the lines are in a bigger font than the others, and bold, and Jim reads one or two of them out loud.

"Do not turn on the flame when your face is directly in front of the Turbo-Tube opening", he says. "WARNING! This gas is not intended for human consumption!"

Then, he tosses the little booklet to the side and says, "We'll just figure it out as we go along."

"Right, Dad!", Bart agrees, admiring his father's sense of no-nonsense thinking and simple logic.

As the afternoon unfolds, there is a lot of cursing, some yelling back and forth between Jim and his son, as well as a couple of band aids being applied... but in the end, there it stands: the "Turbo Charge X-5000", a monument to American industriousness and consumption, with a collapsing condiment tray and its cabinet for dishes and grill tools in easy reach underneath – and all there on Big Jim

Macintyre's backyard patio, for all the world to see and bear witness to.

Well, it's not long before the "inaugural" grill party, at which the guest of honor is more the new barbeque than any of the people who are actually invited.

Among the guests is Mike Jones from next door.

During the party, Mike walks up on the lawn as Jim is standing before the barbeque on the patio, laying cheese squares on the burgers.

"Nice grill", Mike says.

"Thanks!", Jim says, still looking at the orange cheese squares as he lays them, as if the neighbor's observation is just something that he barely notices.

"What's that, the X-5000?", the neighbor asks.

"Yea!", Jim says to the burgers. "Two gas tanks!", he adds, smiling now to Mike and pointing to the tanks below with the tips of his new barbeque tongs.

Then the red robotic lawn mower suddenly charges across the lawn towards Mike's feet, and he steps quickly over it, one foot at a time, to let it go by.

He watches the mower bump tenderly into the edge of the patio, rotate obediently, and then continue onwards.

After it disappears, Mike turns back to the barbeque.

"...nice", he says. Then he takes a bite of his hotdog and raises the remainder of it as a kind of salute, and he leaves Jim and heads back off into the party.

As the corners of the orange squares start to soften, Jim stands there manning the X-5000, smirking at the melting cheese and filled with a sense of satisfaction and accomplishment.

After a busy period at the office (he didn't make it home before 8:00 once this week), Jim starts to celebrate his next Saturday by taking a bag of chips and a drink with him and flopping down onto the chaise lounge on the back patio.

Watching the clouds stretch apart and reshape themselves as he thinks over a few things he has to deal with at work, a big, white point suddenly juts up next door and starts swaying back and forth.

As the point starts to fill out and take form, Jim sees that it is the top of a gazebo – more off-white, actually, or perhaps ivory – being set up in the Joneses' backyard.

With the excuse to himself that he wants to go inside and refill his quart-sized tumbler with more pineapple-chocolate soda and ice cubes, he stands up with a groan and casts a casual glance next door.

The gazebo sticks well above the top of the Joneses' wooden fence, and as a light gust of air starts to blow, Jim sees a long, thin banner with red, white and blue stripes start to unfurl and sway back and forth in the breeze at the tip of the pole above the gazebo.

"Hmm!", Jim says to himself, and he heads inside to the kitchen.

One week passes, and then another, and there are several trips to StuffCo by both Jim as well as his neighbor, Mike Jones.

One afternoon, they actually run into each other by the pool section. Each of their carts is filled to the brim and beyond, and as they chat about their kids and how well their lawns are growing, surreptitious glances are cast here and there at the contents of the other cart – sometimes tactfully, sometimes quite blatantly, and sometimes even with a look of unspoken accusation.

"Puttin' in new border trim by the flower beds, huh?", one of them says.

"Yup", says the other.

At both of their homes, there is a lot of hammering and sawing, sometimes until late into the night. Not much sleep is had, and the number of calls from debt collectors is increasing in both households, proportionally to the amount of yelling and arguments among the spouses.

One evening, sitting on the back patio and going through a stack of mail that he just collected as he came home from work, Jim sees an envelope with a return address for "The Law Offices of Rosenstern and Gildenkranz". He wiggles the tip of his index finger into the opening of the flap and tears the envelop open unevenly.

"Dear Mr. and Mrs. Macintyre", the letter reads, "As your mortgage payments to Mountain Trust Loans, Inc. have been in arrears beyond the previously agreed grace period, a lean will be placed upon your joint income, unless prompt payment is…".

188

A burning sensation develops in his stomach. He takes a few short, sharp breathes, but it is hard to get any air.

As he looks up from the letter with a grimace, he sees a string of lights flash on at either side of the driveway next door.

Instantly, he drops the letter onto the mosaic café table, puts his wet glass of orange cola on top of it, and picks up his smartphone.

He taps onto the Internet, and then accesses the StuffCo website, where he follows the prompts to the heading of "Porch Lighting".

As he searches, his face starts to develop a sly, crooked smile, as the burning in his stomach increases.

Lost

Driving back from a park in another town one day, Kai passes a new housing development on the state road, and in front of the development is a billboard that says "If you lived here, you would be home by now!".

He looks at the sign as he passes by.

'But when I get home, I will also not be here', he thinks to himself, perplexed at the message that the sign is trying to convey.

Lost in thought a bit, he misses his exit and takes the next one a few miles further down, and he ends up in an area that is entirely unfamiliar to him.

The windows in many of the houses are shattered and some are boarded up with plywood, with black and red graffiti scribbled across the wood. One or two windows are covered with stretched-out black garbage bags, stuck onto the deteriorating window frames with grey duct tape.

There are front porches here and there, but the floor-boards of the porches are often broken through, sometimes with jagged, broken planks jutting up in front of the entrance door.

Instead of lawns, there are a lot of tufts of what are mostly weeds, scattered amongst patches of sand and uneven gravel. The homes are also very close to one another and have been built very near to the road.

Kai had never seen anything like this back home in Germany. As he passes, he notices that the mailboxes are all rusty, the paint on the houses is all faded, and there is generally no sign of life to be seen anywhere.

After a series of turns, he ends up on a more populated street, with a few dilapidated store fronts. Up ahead on the side of the road, a man in a cheap T-shirt is walking with the sun baking the brown skin of his arms. He is walking with a casual rhythm to his gate, as if his joints are not limited by tendons and ligaments but contain something more fluid, like butter or rubber bands.

The Euro-expat pulls slowly up next to the man and asks for directions.

"Exkoos me, sir. Can you please tell me how I can get to der main road?", he asks, with a polite smile.

The other man looks through the corner of his eyes without slowing his stride, and when he sees Kai smiling through the open window of his moderate-sized hybrid, the man pauses. Then he knits his eye-brows together and says "You talk kanna funny… wea you vom?", the man says.

Kai sighs as he realizes that he has to inform another person of his personal background in order to continue the conversation.

"I am from Chermany", he says, as he smiles to the man.

"What?! Get da hell outta hea!", the man says, turning half around from the car and laughing out loud. "Germany?", he says, looking at Kai, scowling with his eyes but still with a smile of surprise on his face. "Wachu doon hea?".

For a moment, Kai tries to recall where he might have run across the word "Wachu" in his English studies at the university and what it might mean. Then he pronounces the sounds in his head and responds.

"I sink I have taken a wrong turn, " Kai says, looking at the store fronts across the street.

"Oh, you be on Mahinluta hea".

"Martin Lutter?", Kai says, thinking of the 16th-century Protestant reformist from Germany.

"Yea, Mahinluta. Ya gotta getta Wakanson Avnew."

Kai is not exactly sure of all the words he has just heard, so he asks the man "And where is dat, exactly, sir?".

Then there is a series of sounds that the German expatriate cannot decipher, but the man points one of his arms straight, and then throws his hand to the right, and Kai thinks he knows the way.

"An step on't", the man in the street says, "o' you ain' gonna haf dat lil' ol' shanny cah fo' lon'."

Sitting in his polished hybrid, Kai doesn't know that this brown man walking in the hot sun grew up listening to the rats chewing and scurrying behind the wall next to his bed when he was a child, or that the child's father drank himself senseless after the world around him finally convinced him that he was not actually a person, but something quite less than that, something that didn't count and didn't matter – that after the father left, the boy's mother did what she could to raise him, in the hours when she wasn't at the "Easy Burger" cooking fries or cleaning the few houses that she managed to find work in on the side.

Kai doesn't know that this man's teachers themselves grew up in similar circumstances, and that the text books handed down to the kids from the previous year often had a lot of the pages ripped out, with the books never being replaced. Kai doesn't know that in the jubilant celebration that is American freedom, this man has never received his invitation to the party.

"Sank you," Kai says, and he reaches his palm towards the open passenger-side window to shake hands.

The man in the street pulls his upper torso back intuitively. Then, he looks at the white face in the car, smiles and shakes his own head from side to side.

"Youz one crazy somebitch", the man says,"…but youz awrat."

And they shake hands.

"You too", Kai says, "Yous all right", trying to mimic the new English that he is hearing.

Kai waves as he pulls away, leaving the other man watching him go.

After the green hybrid has driven on a little distance, the other man starts laughing to himself and shaking his head from side to side again, as he continues his long walk down Martin Luther King Avenue.

Values

Big Jim and his son Bart are sitting on a couple of up-turned plastic buckets in the garage, cleaning their guns.

"So howzit goin' in school?", Jim says, looking at the dark, iron barrel as he rubs it with a cloth.

"OK", Bart says, looking away and down at his own gun as he works on it. "Mister John, the Art teacher, showed us some pictures of a coupla paintings the other day. They're from France, a long time ago."

Jim suddenly feels out of his element. After all, as far as he understands it, paintings have nothing to do with acquiring capital or getting ahead of the competition.

"Well, what'd they look like?", he says, taking a shot in the dark with his question.

"They were OK", Bart says. Then after a pause, he looks up at his father and says, "Did you ever see anything like that?".

Jim dips his cloth in some cleaning solvent.

"Sure", he says, "there were a couple of paintings in the hallway at work a few years back, before the big snack machine was put in."

He's starting to be concerned about what they're trying to teach his son now, at that "lefty school", as he calls it.

"But there ain't no money in making pretty paintings, is there, Bart?", he says, his eyes on the cylinder as he cleans its bumpy folds.

"Yea", the boy says, following the path that has been cleared for him. "Art's a waste of time… it's pretty stupid."

Then, Big Jim tilts his head to the side briefly.

"Except for that guy who put those metal tube things in the park that year", he says, on second thought. "Called it an 'installment'…bet he made a *killing* with that stuff", he says, and he holds the back of his gun up to his face and squints one eye as he looks along the barrel to the sight.

"Now THAT'S what I call an artist", he says, clicking the trigger, and he looks at his son, who nods in agreement – message delivered, message received.

"What else are they feeding you at that *school*?", Jim says, making the word "school" sound sarcastic.

"Well", Bart says, "in our 'Future Horizons Workshop', a guidance councilor told us about the 'Caring Professions'".

He looks looks up at his father and continues. "He said you could be a social worker, a teacher, or… or in elderly care."

Jim shakes his head slowly from one side to the other and lets out a light chuckle. As he reaches for a cotton swab to clean out the holes where the bullets go, he says, "Never heard of anybody makin' a good livin' in any of *those* jobs."

Then, he inserts a swab into one of the holes and wriggles it around.

"Unless ya' get inta management", he says. "If ya' run one of them elderly care places, ya' can make a gold mine!"

He tosses the swab at the garbage pail down on the ground. The swab hits the rim and lands somewhere behind the pile of wood that blocks the work bench.

Jim scowls at the garbage pail.

"Boy", he says, "that school is really trying ta' make a patsy outta you kids!"

"Yea!", his son says, sitting defiantly upright all of a sudden, now that a clear direction has been laid out for him.

"There was this poem we had to read in school", Bart says, a little excited now, talking as if he's recounting to a police officer the events leading up to a crime. "It's about a butterfly on a flower, and the flower starts shaking, so the butterfly flies up, and from up above, the butterfly looks down and sees the bad environment, the rivers are all polluted, and there's a big pile of plastic floating in the middle of the ocean."

Bart stops cleaning his gun and looks up at his father, waiting for a reaction.

"Yea", Jim says. "Well, I'd like to see that butterfly try to pay for a mortgage", and they both look at each other and laugh.

"Or the guy who wrote the story, for that matter", Jim adds, not realizing that there is a difference between a poem and a story.

"Yea", his son says, smiling and scowling at the same time, clearly comfortable in his and his father's shared anger at the poem.

Bart knows what he thinks about it now.

"Anyway", Big Jim says, putting down his polished gun before picking up the next one and looking down its barrel, "we got better things ta' do, don't we?".

"Yea!", Bart repeats, smiling defiantly as he looks down the site of his own shiny barrel.

The Fourth of July

"I *lo-o-o-ove* the Fourth of July, dude!", Big Jim says, radiating a glow of ebullience as they pick their way through the crowd.

"Yes", Kai says, who has joined Jim and his family to the parade in town, "I can see why."

The sidewalks on both sides are chock full of people, and the colors of red, white and blue are simply everywhere, in all of their possible combinations: there are busty young women in tantalizing American-flag bikini tops; colorful, floppy Uncle Sam hats with their thick red and white bars and their blue color fields with bold, pointy stars; faces and bare bodies painted in glaring, patriotic revelry; big, round pins, like eyes popping and with the words "Born in the USA!" blaring from them; families in which the husband is wearing red, the wife is wearing white, and the children are wearing blue shirts with white stars on them; and American flags of all sizes – miniature ones stuck into hats, hand-sized flags being held aloft into the air and fluttered jubilantly, quickly back and forth, at the slightest tingling of excitement; and big American-flag beach towels wrapped around women's waists, ready for picnics or pool parties somewhere after the parade.

And there is no end to the variety of T-shirts, proclaiming a wellspring of modern American pride; "AMERICAN and *DAMN PROUD OF IT*!" some say, while others warn "USA: Love it or *Leave It!*". There are shirts with the coiled rattlesnake and the "Don't tread on me!" emblem that had its origins in the American Revolution hundreds of years ago and which had been countermanded by the Tea Party movement a few years back. And there is one that just says, "I'm with Stupid" with an arrow pointing to whoever happens to be standing next to that person at the moment – a good-humored statement of boldness, provocation, playfulness and self-expression that somehow fits into this casual, wild celebration of individuality and freedom.

Jim leads his group to a place up in front on the sidewalk, and through a combination of stretching and turning and expanding himself, he somehow manages to appropriate a bit more space once he has established his settlement.

It's a beautiful day, with a bright sun shining from a clear, blue sky.

"*GREAT* day for a parade!", Jim calls out to the whole world around him.

"Sure is, hon!", Wendy agrees, as enthused by the event's energy and her own Americanness as is her husband.

A vendor passes in the street pushing a cart. It has American flags jutting and protruding from every possible corner.

"Chompy Chips!", the vendor calls out into the crowd. "Get yer Chompy Chips!"

There is a unique kind of conflict within the minds and hearts of the parade watchers as he passes before them, a particularly American kind of conflict – between wanting to give in to their impulses to wallow in the consumption and immediate gratification that the vendor has to offer during this moment between their previous and their next

198

anticipated distraction, and knowing that the goods the vendor is hawking are stunningly overpriced and, therefore, just not a very good deal. And every single American in the crowd teeters on the fine line between these two conflicting urges in their own particular way, as the vending cart rolls past before their eyes and stomachs.

"Ya' want some Chompy Chips?", Big Jim asks his children, blindly regurgitating the advertising name of the product.

"What else they got?", his son asks, and the vendor immediately continues with "Slush Pops. Get yer Slush Pops!"

Then, a man from deep inside the crowd raises his arm high and calls out "I'll take two slush pops!", and Jim whirls his head around at the distraction.

"Cherry o' Grape?" calls back the vendor.

"Uhhh…" the potential customer says, still teetering on that fine line as he looks at his wife. Before she says anything, he instantly explodes with "Grape!", as if he is Albert Einstein suddenly discovering that little missing piece that holds the whole glorious ball of wax together.

"That'll be five bucks!", the vendor calls out, handing the grape slush pops to the nearest person in the crowd. It is just assumed that everyone knows the procedure (which they do), and the slush pops make their way, hand by hand like a baton in a relay race, all the way to the man deep in the middle of the throng of American humanity.

Meanwhile, the man is hurriedly digging in his saggy shorts pocket for his wallet. Finding it, he slips out a worn-down, smooth five-dollar bill, which he hands in complete trust to the first person in front of him who is standing in the direction from which the slush pops are coming.

The vendor and the end customer form two points on a line which is efficiently and economically the shortest distance possible between them. The soft five-dollar bill is passed high in the air from one eager hand to the next, the money reaches the vendor, and the grape slush pops make their way back along the same line to reach the man and his wife.

It's a thing of beauty to behold.

"Alright!", the customer calls out, waving the slush pops to the vendor as much as to the entire crowd, confirming the success of the transaction as well as his satisfaction with the closure of the deal.

"Happy Fourth!" the vendor calls out, and everybody in the crowd is smiling and feeling good about their America and the part they have just played in it.

From down the street, a metallic roar of excitement and intensity is born into the air, and a tremendous frenzy is seen approaching them.

Instantly upon perceiving it, the Americans let loose a cheer of screams and shouts in welcome of the jubilant commotion.

It is a parade float, and along with the blaring music, the float is blazing with the colors of the state football team. There are cheerleaders bouncing and kicking atop of the float, and the team mascot – a giant, hairy orange monster with bulging, angry eyes – is running all over the street, punching his fist into the air and wriggling his giggly body uncontrollably to the music.

The spectators on both sides of the street rummage about as they turn around, and then they take pictures of themselves with the parade float in the background.

Everybody is smiling and laughing to their phones, as if a great moment in their lives has now come upon them – but nobody is actually watching the float or the mascot that are passing by behind them, in the background of their selfies.

The cheerleaders on the float wave their pom-poms ecstatically to the backs of the audience as the music continues to pound, and the mascot writhes his overflowing rotundity in a wild, hairy frenzy, which is captured on countless videos and photos for enthusiastic playback later, although nobody actually watches him directly as he struts around and does his thing.

The float and the mascot tumble and surge onwards, and after everyone has finished looking at their videos of the recorded experience and shown them to each other, they get back to chatting excitedly and waiting for the next big thrill, whatever it might turn out to be.

Towards the back of the crowd, which almost exclusively consists of white people, there is one young black couple and their two children, and all of them are likewise decked out in festive red-white-and-blue attire. They had started up close to the curb when they first arrived earlier in the morning, but over the course of the day, they were slowly but surely pushed to the back of the group, one nudge and one "Pardon me, excuse me" at a time.

"Can I get up on your shoulders, Papa?" the little girl asks her father.

"Uhhh, I don't think that's such a good idea right now, baby", the man tells her, looking around. He likes to pick her up and let her ride on his shoulders in the back yard at home, or when they're visiting friends and family, but not here, not now – after all, there can always be a shooter somewhere, and if he's not too happy with their presence, it can turn out to be too costly for them to call attention to themselves, here on this sidewalk on the Fourth of July.

The chatter in the crowd is interrupted by a few hoots and hollers as the next parade float is noticed coming towards them from down the street.

It's a dance squad, and the young women in it twitch and shake themselves to the overpowering volume of the pop-music that is erupting from the giant speakers at the top of the float. The dancers are adorned in metallic and leather garments which, in any other type of cloth, would be considered string bikinis, and they are pulsing the flesh of their rounded backsides back and forth with the pounding rhythm.

The crowd is screaming is elation, and after the dancers whip their tenuously suspended breasts from one side to the next, they pause robotically and the music goes silent... before the dancers suddenly burst into a choreographed anarchy of throbs and gyrations to the techno-rhythm, as the hooting swells and becomes more uncontrolled and euphoric.

With unwavering attention, Jim's daughter Jasmine is mimicking each and every move and pulsation of the dancers' bodies that she possible can there, in the little space that has been democratically allocated to her on the

202

sidewalk – as are a handful of other teenage girls in the crowd.

In the street, the head dancer suddenly freezes into a pose and she strokes her body, from her upper chest and down her sides to her hips, when she suddenly releases an orgasmic "Pop!" on beat to the music, and the spectators roar is wild support of her sexual liberation and freedom.

Then, as she whirls around, what had until then been a tempting and gratefully viewed display of "side-boob" inadvertently slips, just a little too far, from within its metal and leather confinement, and the celebrants in the boisterous American crowd suddenly find themselves face-to-face with none other than that most unexpected and unwelcomed intruder to their festivity of libertinism – a human nipple.

"*OHHH!!*", members of the crowd shout, turning themselves instantly away and raising their open palms before their eyes, as if blocking their sight from the rays of a burning sun.

"That's dis*gus*ting!!", people scream, as the music is stopped and the woman wraps her bare arms around her chest and cowers in place, looking shamefully from side to side for somewhere to hide her suddenly wayward flesh from the angry mob surrounding her.

"You should be a*shamed* of yourself!", a woman screams.

"There are innocent *children* out here, for God's sake!", a man shouts, raising his fist.

"And on the Fourth of July, of all things!"

"You better pray that God forgives you!", someone shouts vengefully.

And the other dancers surround the "nipple-woman", using their scantily clad bodies to shield her from view and ushering her inside the housing of the float, which whisks her away at top speed (which, for a parade float, is about 15 miles per hour).

The spectators scowl at each other in mutual disgust at how "obscene" the moment of the nipple-slippage was, how "filthy", how "indecent".

As they stand about and whip up their sense of repulsion at such a display of profanity, a car suddenly speeds up in the street and swerves dangerously close to part of the crowd on the sidewalk.

There is a cacophony of wild screams, and everybody there runs from the curb and presses themselves inwards towards the back of the crowd, creating a "V" of emptiness where the car almost made contact.

Then, the car wobbles back and forth before aligning itself and then heading straight down the street and driving away.

"Anybody hurt?", a bold male voice calls out from the crowd, taking charge.

After a pause, somebody responds, "No, everything's cool, he didn't get anybody."

"Looks like he was trying to mow us all down!", a woman's voice calls out.

There is a group of young men a little further down the sidewalk. One of them is wearing a baseball cap that says "USA!" and a worn, grey T-shirt with the words "Live Free or Die!" encircling a picture of an angry bald eagle.

"Probably couldn't see through his burka!", the young man calls out, ostensibly to his buddies, but loud enough for everyone in the crowd to easily hear.

As his buddies laugh, another young man across the street who is wearing hot-red sequinned shorts and tinted sunglasses calls out with a lisp, "It was as old white couple, and they had their grandkids in the back seat".

"Whadda *you* know?", the man with the angry eagle on his chest shouts out across the pavement. "You can't see *anything* through those rose-colored glasses, anyway", and he looks at his buddies and they all laugh together.

"These sunglasses are red-white-and-blue, baby", the other man says, snapping his fingers, to the flamboyant laughter and applause of the two young men he is celebrating with at the parade.

Then, an old man with a big American-flag pin on the side of his floppy, beige fishing hat says, "I may not agree with your opinion, but I respect your right to say it[3]". He recites it into the crowd, factually and respectfully, as if he is speaking from out of another time.

"That's right!", shouts the man in the sequined shorts as he tosses up his head and points to the old man.

Then the guy with the angry eagle on his chest calls out, "You tell that to your grandson, old man, when he comes home one day and says he wants you to start calling him Cindy".

---

[3] The actual quotation by Evelyn Beatrice Hall is "I disapprove of what you say, but I will defend to the death your right to say it".

205

His buddies all laugh wildly, and the old man turns suddenly to his left and stares at his young grandson, who is sucking contentedly on a grape ice pop. The boy's lips are all purple.

Just then, Big Jim plucks out a can of cola that is handed to him from the crowd, raises it in thanks to the passing vendor, and pulls the aluminum tab.

There is a loud "POP!" from the carbon fizz, and everyone nearby turns quickly and cowers for safety – including the two men who have been arguing with each other – afraid that what they just heard was a gunshot from a shooter somewhere.

Oblivious to this result of his actions, Big Jim smiles as he guzzles the high-calorie contents and says, "Ah, now THAT'S what I call a Fourth of July!".

The Feminist

"Is it a bad time?", Wendy's mother says from inside the little square on the television screen.

"Oh", Wendy sighs, "when is it *ever* a good – Jasmine, move over! I can't see your grandma!"

The teenage girl tosses her head up and releases an overly dramatic sigh. Then, she incorporates a smooth side-step to the left into the twitching dance routine that she is mimicking from the infotainment program on the rest of the monitor in front of her.

"It looks like you got a lot piled up there in front of you", the grandmother's image says.

Wendy bugs her eyes out wide and releases a stream of breath as she fumbles around with some dinner items behind the breakfast bar.

"Jim might be home any minute, and he likes ta' eat right away", she says.

There's a pile of unfolded laundry dumped out onto the couch, and next to that is an iron and an ironing board.

The dog barks suddenly out in the yard with a loud "YOWMP!", and Wendy jumps, spilling a can of peas on the counter. The liquid from the can starts to spread, and she steps over the mop that is sticking out on an angle from the bucket as she reaches for the sponge.

"Did you ask Jim about hiring someone to help out a little with the chores, like we talked about?", Wendy's mother says from the little square next to the video of the quivering, jerking pop-stars.

"Well, it's not really a good time for that right now", Wendy says, looking down at the puddle that she is scraping together on the counter.

"Are you having some money problems?", the grandmother asks.

"No!", Wendy says, squeezing the sponge out in the sink and then stepping back over the handle of the mop. "It's just not the right time for us."

The grandmother's eyes shift to the side as they watch Jasmine strut brazenly to the refrigerator and then yank open the door on beat. The girl takes a peeled mini-carrot out of a bag, hurls the door closed with a loud "FLUMP!" and then struts back to the screen, chomping each time she takes a step.

"When *I* was young", the grandmother says to Wendy, with her eyes still cast to the side as she watches her granddaughter dance, "we burned our bras!".

"I know, ma", Wendy says, as she scoops the peas up in her hands from the counter and lets them drip into a serving bowl.

"We protested… we *marched!*", the defiant face in the little square says.

"I know, ma…", Wendy says, impatiently, "heard all about it."

"We went out and *changed the world*", the grandmother says, nodding in self-affirmation.

There is the sound of a car pulling into the driveway.

"Oh, there's Jim. I gotta go, ma!", Wendy shouts at the screen.

"Well, don't forget what I told you", her mother says from the screen, "We came too far to let everything just slip away like –".

"– OK, ma, gotta go, luv ya', bye", and the grandmother is zapped away from the screen, her place taken by a pair of beige, knee-high leather boots worn by a 19-year-old who is dancing as she sings her song that just went platinum.

The front door opens.

"Hi, Sweetheart", Jim says to his daughter, who says "Hi" to the screen without looking away from it.

Then he turns and says "Hey, hon" to the kitchen.

He looks at the television screen and watches the pop star dancing in her tight spandex and tall leather boots.

"Looks like some of the girls at the office", he says.

Day Care

A young mother is standing in front of a day care building, chatting on her phone. She has just picked up her kids, who are already a few feet away from her by this time.

"He did that? Really? And then he didn't even *call* you?", she says in a loud voice as she sneers into the phone.

Her five-year-old boy has a bright blue ribbon clutched in one hand, crumpled up in the middle. He received the ribbon today in the day care program – in recognition of his having started less fights with other children this week than the week before. He has a similar ribbon at home – that one's red, and it has to do with starting fights with teachers.

The boy begins flapping the ribbon at his younger sister (she's three), and he soon moves on to slapping her with it, and then to a certain degree of whipping.

"Logan", the mother shouts at him angrily, with her head turned slightly away from the upheld phone, "stop hitting your sister!".

Then, the mother returns to chatting with her friend and, after a pause that is only as long as the boy knows is necessary, he returns to hitting his sister, with no further interruption from the woman.

After a while, Logan starts to chase his sister in a circle around their mother, occasionally bumping the woman off balance.

Soon enough, though, the boy loses interest in the pursuit; he squats on the ground, looks bored, and then starts throwing rocks at the side of the car that is parked in front of theirs.

Across the street, another little girl is walking on the sidewalk licking a bright, orange lollipop. Logan's little sister sees the lollipop, calls "La-La" out loud to nobody, and starts to waddle towards the lollipop.

As she gets to the edge of her own side of the sidewalk and starts to step unstably into the street, the mother's eyes bulge and she screams "Briana!" into the phone.

As the child starts to topple from the curb into the black street, the mother lunges and grabs the child, pulling her by the arm back to where the mother herself is standing.

Still holding onto her daughter's little hand, the mother returns to the conversation on the phone, but she is distracted by a rhythmic tapping at the legs of her pants.

It's Logan. He has grown bored with the car and has started to throw the stones at his little sister; the stones occasionally miss the little girl and hit the mother's leg.

The woman looks down, sees the event that is unfolding, and says "I gotta go" in a voice of agitated frustration. Then, she taps away her friend and swipes to a children's computer game.

She sticks the phone in front of the boy's eyes and wiggles it back and forth briskly, and he clamps his fingers around it, dropping his crumpled blue ribbon, which slowly blows away from him in the light breeze.

With a big, gaping smile, his little sister staggers over to look at the screen, like a moth drawn to a bright window on a dark night. Then, the mother maneuvers the two children by their shiny, bulbous heads towards the car. They move along without resistance, thoroughly distracted by the changing and shifting stimulations from the mother's phone that has been handed down to them.

… and the legacy continues.

Straightened Out

"She's kind of... peculiar", Anke says in German into her uncle's ear.

Through her wide-lensed glasses, she casts a studious eye upon her American age mate, Jasmine, who is watching her own image in a mirror as she practices a new hair-flipping technique she had seen in a video that morning.

Anke and her parents have come from Germany to visit Kai in the USA, and everybody thought it would be a good idea for the two girls to get to know each other – actually, Kai and his family thought it might make a valuable contribution to Anke's education, to which Jim immediately said, "Yea, that would definitely be *cool!*".

Later, when it's just the other adults together, Kai suggests that Anke join Jasmine to her classes at school, to see what studying in America is like. When Wendy mentions the plans to her daughter, Jasmine grimaces as if she has just smelled rotten cheese and says through her sneer, "That Euro-nerd girl?", followed by a dramatic sigh and eye roll, and then a "whatever" in a tone that is somewhere between exasperation and apathy as she leaves the room.

The next day, as Jasmine stomps her sequined leather boots to her own rhythm through the doorway of her "Cultural Studies" class, all eyes are upon her. She is wearing a short denim skirt and a tight, low-cut top, which leaves little material for support and even less to the imagination.

Her look of total disinterest in those around her has been honed to perfection, and her coinage has been greatly increased ever since the photos of the sudsing at the car wash made the rounds on the Internet.

She doesn't have any books with her, leaving her arms and hands free for some of her more persuasive "I really don't *care* if you look at me!" gestures, which are precisely timed to mesmerize and enthrall.

The heads of the boys in the class all turn as she struts to her desk and pivots, letting the medium that is her own self fall phlegmatically into her chair.

Nobody notices the tall, skinny girl with the brown-rimmed glasses and the books hugged to her abdomen who follows a few paces behind. Anke places her books neatly on the desk next to Jasmine's and sits upright against the back of the chair, and the boys do not hide their efforts to stretch and see around her to their object of fascination.

Surveying her new surroundings, Anke notices the pin-up boards scattered around the room, all covered in brightly colored posters with goofy caricatures of famous historical figures and pedagogical slogans such as "Fun Facts!" and "I Got the Burn to Learn!".

She had looked through the text books at home. Apart from the many cartoons, speech bubbles and crooked little text boxes in various fonts that crowded the page, she was able to glean that the material was two years behind what she had already covered back home in Germany.

As the bell rings, the teacher rushes in, slaps her books on her desk and emits a heavy gasp of air. Then, she laces her handbag over the back of her chair.

She is wearing jeans and a kind of a sleeveless T-shirt, leaving the meaty flesh of her upper arms free.

By this point, most of the kids have already switched to their classroom mode – heads bowed down, looking and clicking at their phones.

"Well", the teacher starts, gathering her wits about her, "Today's a special kinda' day, folks. We got Jasmine's friend visiting us, all the way from *Germany*!".

She smiles to the new girl, who smiles back politely.

"Unka, is it?", the teacher asks, bending her eyebrows over a few papers that are scattered across her own desk.

"It's Anke, actually", the girl says, and smiles again.

"Well, let's all give a nice, warm, American welcome to…Untka."

A few of the students look up briefly from their computer games and their friends' social-media pages and grumble a disinterested, monotoned "Hey". Then, their eyes fall slightly off-target from her onto Jasmine's carefully assembled image of disarray, before returning lethargically to their phones.

"Well", the teacher resumes, "today, we're gonna talk a little bit about the Middle East".

After a groan from the audience, the teacher adds, "Don't blame me; the Superintendent's Office makes me talk about this stuff."

She starts by hovering her finger over the general area where the Middle East more or less is on the world map on the wall beside her, though an inattentive student might easily assume that she is pointing to India.

"And that there's Iraq", she says, looking at a space on the map. "Some of your daddies might remember that we had a little war with them a few years back."

At the mention of the word "war", a couple of boys look up from their phones, but they see the teacher standing in front of her desk talking and they lower their heads back to their screens.

"It's always been a region with a lot of problems", the teacher explains. "A lot of aggression, a lot of anger against us, way over here in America."

The new visiting student from Germany raises her hand straight and high, and the teacher smiles at this welcome novelty of class participation.

"Yes, the new girl… Unka!", the teacher says, smiling eagerly as she points to her.

Smiling in return, Anke says, "Actually, the land where Israel now is used to belong to the Palestinians, before it was taken from them, particularly by the US and the UK." Anke has her hands folded atop her desk. "Perhaps that is why people in the Middle East are angry at the West."

The teacher just stands at the front of the class and looks at the student, without speaking. She is not used to challenge in the classroom – at least not when it's comingled with attentiveness and insight.

"Wuh, well", the teacher stammers, walking back behind her desk, where she feels more in control of things, "they needed a place for all the Jewish people, after the Second World War".

216

Assuming the matter to be settled, she turns back to the map and starts to continue with her presentation, when she again hears the slight German accent of the girl from the middle row.

"But they could have been allowed to immigrate to America", the girl says, in the impeccable English that is common to her more well-educated age mates in her home country. "In fact, there was a ship with hundreds of Jewish refugees who wanted to enter the US in the late 1930s, and the US immigration office turned them down."

The teacher stands and looks back at the calm face of the young girl, who is clearly waiting for a logical rebuttal of some kind.

Receiving none and seeing that the teacher is just standing there staring at her, the girl adds, "It was the M.S. St. Louis in 1939. They were sent back to Europe, and a lot of them were murdered later."

"Well", the teacher says, picking up a wooden pointer from the metal rack under the white board. "I don't know where you get your information from, Miss", and there is a pause, as the teacher tries to recover lost ground, "but we had to do a lot of things back then because of that *German*, Adolf Hitler". As she accentuates the word "German", she looks out at the foreign girl who is presenting these questions, questions that are falling well beyond the teacher's grasp.

Anke looks around the room to let somebody else respond. Seeing nothing but the bowed heads around her, and Jasmine looking into her own cosmetics mirror, Anke says, "Uhhmmm, actually, ma'am, Adolf Hitler was born in Austria."

The teacher's eyes bulge somewhat at this new information.

Then, she walks behind her desk and says, "Yes, of course... but, ahhhhh...", groping for a response, "...but it was the Germans who ripped those people out of their homes and forced them to labor, under terrible, inhuman conditions."

Feeling safe in the new line of attack she has found, the teacher smiles deviously and adds, "I mean, what kind of people do that?".

"Yes, that was terrible, without any doubt", Anke says, lowering her eyes a bit. Then she looks up and adds, "Isn't that also what happened to black people in America during slavery?".

There is a sudden chortle from one of the few other students who have by now started to follow the exchange. Another of them has begun to live-stream the verbal confrontation online. Among the other students who are simulating acts of theft and murder as they play computer games on their phones in class, a few of the kids are amazed at this new member in their group; they are astonished at the knowledge she has about the outside world – the world beyond their isolated geographical and intellectual bubble.

Jasmine is not one of them. She continues to look bored and rather aggravated at this babbling about far away places that apparently have nothing whatsoever to do with her.

Clearly stumbling for some firm footage, the teacher says, "Oh, come on now, the Holocaust was much worse."

"I don't know", the girl says, folding her arms and looking reflectively into the air around her. "They were *both* horrible. Murder? Rape? One group dominating another against their will? I guess it doesn't matter which was worse. But I don't think either country is in the position of bragging, after what they've done".

"Now see here", the teacher says, bending forwards and aiming the tip of the wooden pointer sharply at the 16-year-old at the little desk. "We've had a few bumps along the way", the teacher adds. Then she turns and begins walking towards the light from the window with her head up high. "But America's still the most powerful country in the world, and it has been a beacon on a hill for countless generations!".

As she says this, a few of the students who have been following the exchange start to sit more upright. They smile at the teacher, glad that their beliefs, which have been challenged by this intruder, are being propped back up for them.

"America certainly has its positive aspects", Anke says. "They led the rebuilding of Europe after the Second World War, for example, and then they beat the Soviet Union at the Cold War that followed. And there were all of those immigrants who worked their way up into the middle class over the years."

The teacher smiles with satisfaction, tapping the wooden pointer in the palm of her hand.

"But America had its own interests in all of that, natu-rally", the girl says, looking up again and to the side. "I mean, it certainly wasn't out of love for anybody," and Anke laughs lightly at the optimistic notion she herself has just mentioned.

"Besides", she adds, "there have been some things that a lot of Americans don't even know about", Anke adds fac-tually, "things they probably would not be so proud of."

"Like what?!", the teacher scoffs with a throaty laugh, as if challenging the girl to the impossible.

"For example, there was the Tuskegee study, in which black citizens were infected with syphilis by the U.S. gov-ernment, on purpose, just to study the effects on them… while those citizens were told they were getting free medi-cine", the visitor states.

The teacher just stares at her, her own face slack, as if watching a documentary about something she has never seen before, one that places everything in a completely different perspective. Her mouth is gaping a bit, the point-er hanging loosely in her hand.

"Then, there was the MKUltra operation", Anke adds. "That was when the government exposed its own citizens to LSD for research, *again* without telling them."

After a pause, during which the visiting student is at-tentively waiting for a cogent response, the teacher turns around slowly from the class and gently places the wood-en pointer back on the metal tray, where it makes a little series of rattles and clicks.

Then she turns to her handbag that has been dangling from the back of her chair.

"Like I said", the teacher states, with a sudden calm to her voice. She reaches into her bag and lifts out a silver revolver. She feels the weight of it in the palm of her hand.

"We've had a few bumps along the way", the teacher says, and then, pointing the gun towards the American flag hanging in the corner of the classroom, she adds "but America's still the greatest country in the world."

The student who had been live-streaming the argument online sinks down into his chair, as he raises his phone up above the person's head in front of him, hoping to capture the next big online event as it happens – live.

"We still have our rights", the teacher says, wiggling the gun in front of her as some kind of example somehow, "and I thank God for His watching over us here."

She takes a pious glance upwards, and then she glares down at Anke in the middle row, as if suddenly empowered.

"Especially when some *others* try to get people all *confused,* confused about what's *right* and *wrong*", the teacher adds, tapping her two fingertips on the barrel of the pistol, and glowering at the foreign child who has challenged her with logic and facts.

The middle-aged woman standing in front of the class has a tight, haunting look to her face – like someone getting riled up for a lynching.

Anke sits firmly and attentively in her seat. Though not budging an inch or a centimeter from her position in the dialogue, her sharp eyes watch the tip of the gun barrel…

…and she gulps.

Then, she takes a deep breath of the stagnant classroom air on this, her first day of education in the land of the free.

Dinner and a Movie

Big Jim steps up to the snack counter at the movie theater.

"Howyadoin'?", he says to the young man behind the counter.

"Great, howyadoin' today?"

"Great, I'll ta-a-a-a-ake, a-a-a-a-a-a", he drones, with his mouth gaping as he looks up over the young man's head at the giant sign that lists all the snacks he can buy.

The worker looks at the dark whole of Jim's mouth as he waits for the order.

"Uhmmm, I'll ta-a-a-a-a-ake, a-a-a-a-a-a... Super-size Bucket-o-Pop-Corn, a big box a' Choco-Wonka Chips, a-a-a-a-and..."

Suddenly, Jim is distracted by another worker at the other end of the counter, who spins around and positions a customer's gigantic garbage-pail container full of popcorn below a shiny, silver pump. As she presses the handle, a thick, gelatinous, orange-yellow substance oozes out, shimmering in the fluorescent lighting of the movie theater lobby. It coats the popcorn in a dense layer, like a shellac.

"Ooh", Jim says, "what's that yellow stuff? I want somma that!".

How Bouta' Nice Cup a' Coffee?

Up ahead on the corners of the main intersection, Kai sees a crowd of people. They're gathered densely together on either side of the street, raising their fists and screaming as they poke some kind of objects up into the air.

'Are those pitch forks?', he wonders, concerned that his medium-sized hybrid might not be secure enough in case there is some kind of riot.

The traffic light turns red, and he sees the mobs on opposite corners lean in together as two distinct masses towards the stopped cars to shout at them.

Closer now, Kai sees that what they are holding are signs, in bright red, white and blue color fields, and the signs all have political slogans on them.

"Vote for McGillian!"

"Rick Harris: *for* the People!"

"John King: Change Now!"

The same signs are also jutting out at different angles from the ground around them, like grave markers for the politicians they mention.

Kai presses the two levers on the side of the car door to close the windows. He is pushing so firmly that his fingertips are turning white around the nails, and the windows raise at what for the European expat suddenly seems like a frighteningly slow pace.

As he rolls ever so cautiously up to the last free space at the traffic light, he looks through the glass of his closed windows at the screaming faces, as if he is in a zoo, not yet sure which side would be the inside of the cage and which would be the outside.

As they scream at him, they are strangely enough all smiling, flapping their palms as they wave to him, bending over to peer into his car to look him in the eye, calling out, "Hi!", "Hello-o-o!", "Whoo-WhOOO!", "Hey, there!!" and other American greetings, as they pump their political messages up and down.

They all have different signs, and they each act as though their particular candidate is that special, wonderful, fresh, new leader who will revolutionize the world for them. None of the signs have anything particular to say, though, other than the most generic statement that one could have on a sign and it still to be somehow political. If the slogans were any less substantial, they would read something like, "Vote for Johnson – he drinks water!".

The people are so excited and inspired in their waving, sign pumping and shouting, and Kai wonders what they hope to achieve.

'Do they actually think that saying hello to me is a convincing political argument?', he wonders, as he stares back at them, curious and with no expression, like at a group of exotic animals now. 'Is that how they choose their leaders? A stranger said he liked me at the intersection today, so I will select that person's politician and his tax plan?'.

The traffic light turns green, the cars start to slowly pull away, and it looks as though the screamers are waving farewell, to their dear friends from the intersection, who have stopped and been part of this *awesome* political discourse with them today.

225

They each bend and shove their waving palms as close as they can to the cars, as if to say, "We love you! Don't forget, now. Our guy's the best!", and Kai looks straight ahead at the road in front of him, trying not to notice the intrusive behavior of the caterwauling strangers on either side of him.

He's been starting to feel a bit tired with all of the hysteria, all of the irrational exuberance of his new country. He doesn't know if it is homesickness exactly, or perhaps something deeper.

Up ahead, next to "Sofas R' Us!", there's a sign for a café. Kai remembers sitting with his friends and family outside of little Italian ice cream shops back home in Germany and enjoying an espresso or a hearty cup of coffee, with the light breeze passing as he looked up at the old buildings that had survived the war and still had their centuries-old charm.

He turns into the parking lot, files his hybrid among the towering walls of the various SUVs, and walks to the one storefront among the countless others just like it which, in this case, says "World o' Coffee!" at its entrance.

As he opens the doors, along with the burst of cold air from the air conditioning, there is a tumultuous wave of noise from the coffee machines, the hustling "baristas" and the mechanical churning of the cash registers, all layered upon an endless and indistinguishable series of electronic beeps and moans.

The workers behind the counter are jostling about as if they are on fire, trying to keep up with the frenetic pace, doing everything they can as quickly as possible, and then pushing themselves even further, to ensure that the customers are served, as well as to try to escape the grasp of their own encroaching poverty.

In spite of the various chocolate-colored easy chairs and couches positioned here and there in the dining area, it is hardly an atmosphere of leisure – and there is no light breeze. In place of old-world charm, it reminds Kai of a more hectic version of the furniture outlet next door.

He steps to the counter. In front of him in line is an old man ordering, and the man has to yell over the noise in order to be heard. As he shouts his order into the attentive face of the worker, the old man's yellowed teeth are exposed, and his bushy eyebrows knit down into a kind of rug above the bridge of his prominent nose.

It looks and sounds as if he is fighting with the worker, but she just smiles as she takes his order. Then, she says to the old man, "That'll just take a coupla seconds, sir", smiling back to him. She then turns instantly, slaps a slip of paper in front of the coworker behind her at the coffee machine, and pivots back around as she turns to Kai.

The "barista" is about 20 years old, covered with various pins and tags that say "Coffee To Go!", "Hot and Fresh!", and just the provocative word "Croissant?".

"Hi, how can I help ya' today?", she says to Kai, in a tight, high-pitched voice. She looks like she is eager to please, but she is rushing so fast in everything she does, as if she is trying to escape being eaten alive by a school of hungry piranha.

While he places his order, Kai looks past the "barista" and watches her young coworker at the coffee machine; he is pushing the buttons of the machine with a tremendous speed and certainty, like a computer programmer trying hurriedly to defuse the mechanism before it blows him and the entire neighborhood to pieces at any moment.

The young man is working the cups and the dispenser as if it is a magical, technological cow – a "Smart Cow", perhaps. From the thundering, mechanical Smart Cow, a stream of foam flows out like from a fire extinguisher, with an overpowering, whooshing sound. It is all very distracting, and Kai feels a headache developing rapidly as he shouts over the noise to place his order.

The female "barista" asks for Kai's name, rings up the order, repeats to him her sentence "That'll just take a coupla seconds, sir" with the required smile, and then whips around to the coffee machine behind her.

She pats the new slip of paper onto the workspace in front of her colleague, then collects the steaming cup for the previous order, which is ready now – a purely American example of efficiency in sequenced planning and movement, and all for barely above the minimum wage.

She then whirls back around to the counter (there's a lot of whirling in such establishment in America – like in an hysterical ballet). The "barista" then reaches naturally for where she knows the cinnamon canister will be (since everything is precisely located and streamlined, for the sake of efficiency and the customer's satisfaction). She holds a plastic form over the mug and dabs the canister at the foamy top, where a light-brown heart appears and takes shape.

The old man who has been waiting for this cup of coffee approaches the counter, and as he leans over towards it, closer than a customer normally would, he suddenly sneezes, with an excess of volume and a dramatic sweeping of his arms.

He then starts to complain vociferously to the young worker at the counter who is handing him the coffee.

"What's *wrong* with you?!", he shouts at her, "You didn't have to create a Desert Storm with the cinnamon. I'm allergic, for God's sake!"

He doesn't say what he is allergic to, exactly, but he nevertheless continues with his performance.

"I have breathing problems.", he adds. "What are you trying to do, *kill* me?!"

"I'm sorry, sir!"

"You're not supposed to put *that* much cinnamon on top!", and the old man starts coughing, as he pulls out his phone and starts scrolling through a menu, saying "Where's my doctor's number? Forget it, I'm going to call my LAWYER!", and he starts to record a video, aimed at the foamy cappuccino.

He begins to narrate the video by saying "I'm standing here, at the coffee shop, and this woman is trying to KILL me!"

"I'm *so-o-o* sorry, sir!", the young woman says, bowing somewhat to him as she presses her hands together in front of herself, as if she is praying.

"I've got serious respiratory problems, and she's just *throwing* cinnamon powder all around the place… and I know my rights. I have the right to come here and get a cup of coffee without having to take my LIFE in my hands, just because…"

With a look of fear on her face, the young worker at the counter tries desperately to placate the bitter, old man.

"I'm sorry, sir. I'm sorry", she continues. "Why don't you accept this one on the house?", and she hands the hot, foamy cappuccino with the little cinnamon heart on it to the cantankerous old customer.

The old man grumbles discontentedly, saying something about being "more careful next time!" as he takes his free coffee, and he goes and sits with his paper cup at one of the tall seats at the bar, alone.

Watching the old man slump in front of the window and scowl out at the SUV's in the parking lot, Kai suddenly hears the young woman shout out "Kite? Kite!" into the body of the store.

After a slight exchange of questioning glances and friendly nods between himself and the young woman behind the counter, it is established that the coffee is in fact his. He takes his cup, pays for it with a tired smile, and goes to take a seat at a table.

Next to him, a guy in a baseball cap at another table is playing a video from a news program on his phone. It's a financial program, and the voice of the presenter shouts angrily from the little speaker "…and they conveniently forget that without Wall Street, there wouldn't even *be* a Main Street!".

From another table near the window, another man who is sitting in front of a frothy orange drink says to the man watching the video, "That reporter doesn't care that he's owned by a big corporation, who probably told him exactly what to say in that video." As he says it, he smiles to the other man, as though he is glad to be entering into a pleasant conversation with him.

The man with the baseball cap looks up from his phone and stares at the man with the frothy drink.

"It's the corporations that keep this country alive", the man watching the video says.

The other man looks out the window and laughs. "Ya' call this living?", he says, bending to sip his drink.

The man watching the video eyes him, and then says, "It's a lot better than in them other countries, where they got the government tellin' 'em what to do all the time."

Smiling to him, the man with the frothy drink sighs unnaturally and says, "I wish *some*body would tell these big companies how to stay in line. Maybe we wouldn't have so many people struggling to keep their heads above water."

"Well", the other man says, frowning, "anybody who don't like it can get the hell out any time they want to!".

"Oh, that's typical", the other man says, turning towards the other table."If you don't like Wall Street raping you, keep your mouth shut and go away. Nice!"

The man watching the video repositions himself, sitting closer to the edge of his seat. "Well, if ya' want everyone ta' get some kinda handout, then why don't ya' go make a coupla million and give 'em everything ya' have, instead of sittin' around and drinkin' frappuccinos all day long?", he says.

"Health care is a hand out?", the other man responds, still with a tone of artificial friendliness and a posed smile.

"If ya' ain't workin' ta' afford it, you bet it is!", the other man says, clutching his phone in a fist. "This is a free country, and that's why so many people swim across the ocean to get to us."

Sitting a few tables away, Kai remembers the glass of wine he drank on the plane on the way over. It was a Merlot.

"Those immigrants have to swim through the dead bodies of all the people who don't survive the trip", the man with the frothy orange drink says, his tone now elevating as he scowls at the other man. "It's disgusting!"

"I'll tell you what's disgusting!", the man in the baseball cap shouts back at him, pounding on the table top. "People crowdin' us out of our own country who don't belong here. Now *THAT'S* disgusting!"

"Hummph!", the other man says, tossing his head up into the air judgmentally.

The man with the playing video raises up his fist and then juts out an index finger to point at the man at the other table. "We gotta be careful with government tellin' us how to run our own business", he shouts. "We don't need people over there in Washington tellin' us what to do!"

"We don't need Washington to sell us out, either!", the man shouts back, grabbing hold of his frothy drink, as if about to throw it at his adversary and unleash all of the wrath and fury that a cool frappuccino is capable of.

Quietly sipping his coffee, Kai notices that the men didn't say Washington, D.C., and he wonders if either of them know that they are actually fighting about a state in the north west, across the country from there the White House is located.

The two men stare hatefully at each other, from across the political divide in this landscape of café tables, latte and other foamy beverages.

From the phone of the man in the baseball cap, the video is coming to an end. The metallic voice from the little speaker can be heard saying, "...in this, the greatest country in the world".

Kai takes another sip of his coffee.

'That's it', he finally decides then and there, 'I'm going back to Germany'.

About the Author

Jonathan Claay is an incredibly good looking guy who has everything going for him. Women love him, and guys love to be around him.

He has lived and worked in numerous countries, lived a generally wild life, and learned a number of foreign languages to varying degrees.

He is currently creating a new computer app: when a person just touches a button on it, they will become instantly happy, forever.

About the Book

(fiction)

Did you hear the story about the European who moved to America?

America – that potpourri of modern dysfunctionalia...

> ...that sticky, spicy, simmering crawfish gumbo of a society...

> ... where a half-white man can become the first black president.

America – love it or leave it... or *else!*